GAIA
-2045-

Spring 2021

for Jackie Davis
a superlative English
teacher! X 2 !!!

♡

SUSAN REINTJES

Susan
Reintjes

BALBOA.PRESS
A DIVISION OF HAY HOUSE

Balboa Press books may be ordered through booksellers or by contacting:

Balboa Press
A Division of Hay House
1663 Liberty Drive
Bloomington, IN 47403
www.balboapress.com
844-682-1282

Print information available on the last page.

ISBN: 978-1-9822-5338-7 (sc)
ISBN: 978-1-9822-5337-0 (hc)
ISBN: 978-1-9822-5348-6 (e)

Library of Congress Control Number: 2020916044

Balboa Press rev. date: 10/13/2020

Dedicated to Dorothy Maclean, pea plant whisperer,
explorer of unseen worlds and author of *To Hear the Angels Sing*.
And to Rachel Carson, author of *Silent Spring*,
who knew and spoke out to warn us all.
This is our last chance.

Bees are the batteries of orchards, gardens, guard them.
—Carol Ann Duffy, *The Bees* (2011)

If the bee disappeared off the face of the earth, man would only have four years left to live.
—Maurice Maeterlinck, *The Life of the Bee* (1901)

The Caterpillar on the Leaf
Repeats to thee thy Mothers grief
Kill not the Moth nor Butterfly
For the Last Judgment draweth nigh
—William Blake, "Auguries of Innocence" (1863)

CONTENTS

CHAPTER 1

KNEELING IN A STAND OF poppies, I am surrounded by swarms of insects dancing on the red blooms. I scoop up handfuls of winged beings and put them into my mouth. Without swallowing, I keep piling them in until the gentle buzz of my ward wakes me up.

My ward is never awake this early. It's still dark and the others are sleeping, heads buried under covers. My ward is restless and needs air and I need sleep to escape from my thoughts. My ward wins. She is one of a rapidly dwindling number of her species. We've been together for three years and my sole purpose is to guard her kind from extinction. We've grown so close that we can read each other's thoughts and predict each other's movements.

As I move through the grounds, the tickle of her tiny feet warns me that my ward is on the move. The sleep pod in my shirt is always open so that she can come and go, but she knows to stay close. We need each other. My ward surfaces, her tiny head covered with black and yellow fuzz. Looking right and left, she senses the night air and her furtive glances quicken. I catch my ward's alertness as gooseflesh rises on my neck.

Wanting deeper contact, I lift a palm to my chest and invite her to ride on my hand. She agrees and I bring her up to my forehead. The buzzing heightens and bursts of electric pulses reach my pineal gland. She moves to the crown of my head and sends her signals deep into my brain. Someone is near, someone unexpected. I stop, but my ward signals me to keep walking. I'm confused, but I obey her. I have learned to never override her directives. We each know the protocol. My ward will take flight and I will use my wits to evade capture. I would rather die than endanger my ward. She is my purpose. I have no other desire than to keep her alive.

I veer right toward the pond and my ward pulls me back into a straight line. Her command is to go straight ahead, which puts us heading toward the gate. I fight off fear by remembering I must always trust my ward's instincts. She knows best. When we arrive at the gate, the night air is still and breathless. My ward detects the pounding in my chest. She doesn't feel fear and comforts me whenever I emit fear pheromones. "It's okay." That's all she says. How can it be okay when I know a stranger is near in the middle of the night? I resist the impulse to place her back in the pod. She paces on my scalp and the tickling sensation sends chills down my arms. I am not good at waiting.

"It's okay." She repeats it to calm me down. I take deep breaths because I can't do anything else. She's in charge and I am at her service and so we wait. Minutes pass and I tremble, not from tension, but from suspense. My ward continues to pace, pausing now and then to read the air and reassure me.

She lifts off at the same instant that I hear the distant drone of a car. Hovering above me for only an instant, she darts over the gate. The vehicle pauses for a moment and moves on. My lungs deflate and I fall to my knees, my forehead dropping to the ground to meet the earth's pulse. Before I register the full extent of panic and loss, my ward's feet land on my head.

Taking a deep breath, I stand up, signal my relief and wait for her response. She rests in the exact center of my head, emitting a strange chatter. I lift a palm to the top of my head and the tiny pads that touch my hand are not my ward's. Quivering, I bring my hand down to eye level and stare into the eyes of a new young queen bee. She is as curious and startled as I am. I smile at her and she buzzes back in a chaotic pattern. It will take time to learn each other's language.

The wake-up alarm is ringing. Or is this a dream? I awaken to silence and empty beds all around me. Everyone is already in training, except me. Why did they let me sleep through the alarm?

Oh, yes, a guardian always sleeps in when her new ward arrives. I sink back into the mattress, close my eyes and listen to the faint drone of my new queen. I don't understand her yet and I'm curious to know what she's trying to tell me, but for now I'll just rest a little bit longer.

I'm up and dressed, carrying my new ward inside the pod over my heart. I want to throw myself into learning all I can about her, but I miss Q. They tell me she went over the gate to help start a new hive and that she'll be back. I want to settle back into my routine and get back to training. I can't afford to miss any more drills. More new wards will be arriving and we need to be ready. If a delivery is followed, the Compound could be compromised and we need to be prepared for any possible threat.

I know that Hasta is eager to get her moth and butterfly cocoons and Wen's praying mantises need more males to mate with and eat. And Sage wants more ladybugs and...

My watch interrupts my thoughts with a gentle pulse. I look down and read an order to come to the Commander's office. Reluctant to leave my team behind at the training ground, I change direction and move quickly toward headquarters. Commander Stewart is busy at her desk when I arrive, so I wait outside the door until she calls me in.

"Gaia, come in. We are pleased with the arrival of your new ward. You know that more wards arrive in the next few days. Your team is being prepared now, but we have something else for you to do. The new queen is not ours to keep. She needs to go to Scotland and we want you to take her."

I am to be the emissary for a queen? A rush of adrenaline shoots through my blood. At fifteen, I'm to deliver a queen!

"We know that you're the best one to do this and that you can pass all the barriers. You know how strict the laws are concerning insect possession and transport. A trainer is arriving tonight to teach you everything that you need to know to escape detection."

"Yes, Commander."

The adrenaline finally reaches the reasoning part of my brain. Scotland? Escape detection? This sounds serious. I've never left the Compound, so I have no idea how to pass any barriers. I've never been outside the gate. The one time my mother lifted me up on her shoulders, I saw the treetops on the other side of the wall. I remember her holding me close afterwards and the hum of her ward inside her shirt. Wait. Wasn't it in Scotland that my mother disappeared? Oh God, I can't leave the Compound.

When I was scared, I used to ask her what to do and then after she left, I asked Q. And now Q is gone. How can I travel that far without them? But I can't afford to process any of this right now. I need to focus and hear my orders. Thank goodness, the Commander is not a sentient and can't read my thoughts.

"We need to prepare you for your trip. Port City has powerful Mind Inquisitors and they will be expert in overriding any attempt to hide your identity. The MIs are on the lookout for rebels with any connection to the Naturist Cause and they will do everything in their power to intercept and destroy any wards and arrest their emissaries."

As I watch, the Commander turns away from me and looks out the window. The wind seems to react to her gaze and rattles the glass to emphasize her words. Shivers run up and down my back.

"You were selected, not only for your sentient powers with insects, but because you're gifted at Mind Command. You'll start your instruction tomorrow with your trainer, Quince. She'll teach you how to use Mind Command to protect your true memories and build a solid, impenetrable memory overlay. The memory overlay hides your true identity while giving you a new one that doesn't know about the existence of our Compound. You will protect your Gaia identity and allow the cover identity to take you to Scotland."

"Remember the Mind Inquisitors' job is to stop you from delivering the queen. They are stationed at every port of exit and entry. Expert at mind reading, they can detect false identities. Don't worry, Quince will make sure that your new identity is strong enough to block them. The MIs will also try to use your fear backlog to override a memory overlay. You'll need an intensive float session to clear out as many fears as possible. You will have twelve hours in the float first thing tomorrow to let your fears move through you and out. Don't stop the fears when they come up. Stay with them and see them through."

Mind Inquisitors? Memory overlay? Fear backlog? I don't understand any of this, but I do love the float tank. I am weightless and alone in the dark quiet surrounded by warm water, heavy with salt. It's so relaxing, until my fears come up, my strange and terrifying fears. Fears I didn't even know I had. After they crawl through me, they sink to the bottom of the tank and are sucked out through the drain. When I finish, I feel so clear. Four hours is the longest I've done, so twelve sounds like a marathon. Will I be even clearer afterwards or could I end up being emptied out? Will I still remember all that I've learned? The Commander's voice startles me back into the room.

"Remember, don't discuss your mission with any of the others for now, except for Quince. After today, your team training is suspended. Jasper will drive you as far as Port City on the next new moon and then you'll be on your own. You may go now."

The Commander moves to the door and opens it wide. I nod and make the sign of respect: palms facing up with little fingers touching. I leave, closing the door behind me softly. On my own in the world? My new ward's wings brush my cheek on her way to my crown. My nerves immediately respond to her touch and, taking a deep breath, I rush to training.

"Where have you been? I've never seen you sleep so deep." Hasta is dripping with sweat from the morning run when I find her by the pond.

"Did I miss the run?" My shoulders droop in disappointment before she answers me. My whole being registers the unmistakable fatigue of missing a workout. I love running with my team.

"Yes, you know you did. What have you been doing? You couldn't have slept that long!"

"No, I've been up." I want to tell her about the mission. But I can't.

Hasta raises her left eyebrow, waiting for an explanation, and I sidestep her the only way I know. "I don't understand Rani. It's like she's speaking a completely different language than Q."

"Rani?"

"I named her after the Warrior Queen Rani Durgavati. Remember in history class we read about her going to battle when resisting the Mughal invasion in India in the sixteenth century?"

"Not really. But then you're always remembering stuff like that. Do you think she's confused? Or sick?"

"No. I think she's just different than Q. Maybe we need more time together."

"We've got work in the fields today. Are you going to drop Rani off at the hives?"

"No. I think she should stay with me for a bit. She can explore the fields while I weed." I want to tell Hasta about Scotland. I need to tell someone. So, I tell Rani. "We're going to Scotland!" Q would have reassured me, understanding my strange blend of excitement and fear. All Rani says is "Shhhhhhhhh."

CHAPTER 2

WEEDING IS MY FAVORITE WORK duty. Mindless and satisfying, I can let my thoughts go anywhere. While I work, I sometimes imagine the outside world. Even though I love life here, I can't help but wonder about the world outside the gate. Is it like a larger Compound with even more beauty? Or is it dry, dead and desolate like the rumors we hear?

I can hear the others nearby, laughing over something that Sage said. I'm off by myself because I'd rather work alone than fight off the urge to share my news. Hasta knows something's wrong and I can tell that she's worried that I'm mad at her. I left a sprig of lavender on her pillowcase last night so she'll know it's not her, it's me.

Pull and drop. Pull and drop. The pile of weeds grows as my thoughts pile up inside me. I'm going to leave the Compound. How can I get ready to be in a world I've never known?

Looking up from my work, the girls come into view: Trea, Hasta, Sage and Wen. We were all born here. Midwife Amey saw to our safe entry and Doc Becca monitors our health. Our births are not recorded, so we can ride under the radar our whole lives and become whoever we want if we ever do go out into the world. Hack is Trea's nickname because she is a whiz with computers. She can plant cover identities and find anything on the web that we need for security. The Compound would not survive without her.

Hasta is my best friend. She's two years younger than me, but no one would guess it. We are the same height and build. Sometimes I'm the little sister and sometimes she is. It depends on what's happening in our lives. Hasta keeps the dragonflies, butterflies and moths happy. They love her and follow her everywhere. They'll even follow her into the dining hall to perch on her shoulders and hair. Once I woke up to find her bed completely covered in butterflies. At first, I thought I was dreaming until two butterflies left her bedspread and landed on my arm. She slept through it all and by the time she woke up, they were gone. I told her about it and she grinned, blushed and hid her face, like I had caught her kissing a boy.

None of us knows anything about boys, because there aren't any boys or men on the Compound. I do miss boys sometimes, even though I don't even know for sure what I'm missing. The only kiss I've ever had was in a very vivid dream. I don't remember what he looked like, but it was a really sweet kiss and it made me want more. But I'd rather have my life on the Compound than a boyfriend, if I had to choose. I don't know if Hasta likes boys, girls or both. We've never talked about it. I love Hasta and I know she loves me too, but I dream about boys. I don't know who she dreams about. I hope it's not me, because I love her so much that I don't ever want to hurt her. Not ever.

I manage to avoid the team all day by signing up to do the evening feeding for the animals in the barn. I finish with the goats just in time to watch the fireflies appear, one by one, then disappear and reappear. There are so many fireflies this summer that I scarcely need a light to get back to the barracks. I like to predict their flight patterns and I'm getting pretty good at it.

Sage is the guardian of the fireflies and we are all jealous of her. She tells us it's like having fairies as your friends. Distant thunder rumbles and I quicken my step to get back to the barracks. When a storm is approaching the fireflies gather close together and synchronize their lights until they flash as one unit. I like to think our team is like that. When an outside threat arrives, we will strobe together as one force.

All of us together nurture and protect the Compound. It is our only directive. We are mother and father to every being here. The Compound is green, vibrant and teeming with life. Our climate is mild and accommodating, perfect for hosting and preserving as many forms of insect life as we possibly can. The insect world is so smart and in tune that more species arrive here every day, on their own, seeking shelter. They know instinctively where they will be guarded and can thrive.

I wasn't alive when insects were legal, but the elders remember and they tell us stories about towns with fields of wildflowers thick with bees, acres of fruit orchards filled with butterflies and ponds dotted with translucent dragonflies. I wish I could have seen that, but I know I was born into a very important time. One day, our Compound will repopulate the world with our insect friends and helpers.

Rani wakes me up by buzzing from her resting place in my ear. It's still dark outside and the others are sleeping when I pull on my clothes and leave for the marathon float. I want to crawl back into bed with Rani, but instead I leave her pod on my pillow with her inside. Outside the air is crisp and invigorating. Frogs and crickets are calling out to possible mates and answers float back through the night air. A few stars are still visible in the night sky and I make a wish. "I wish for the Compound to stay safe and healthy." I breathe in deeply and exhale sending the message out into the ether. I whisper, "Keep me safe, too," in preparation for the long float ahead of me.

I let myself into the float hut and start my routine by hanging my sweats on a peg on the wall. The shower is lukewarm, strong and steady, and the soap is peppermint and stings a little. I scrub all over, from my hair to my feet. When I'm rinsed, I open the tank lid, slide into the warm salt bath and pull the top down.

Complete darkness enfolds me, the kind of darkness that is darker than night. Whether my eyes are closed or open, it looks exactly the same. The water matches my body temperature so I can hardly register where it touches me. My face, breasts and thighs float above the surface. The first time in the tank I tried to submerge my whole body, but the salt wouldn't let me. And the next time, I was afraid of going under if I fell asleep so I got a stiff neck tensing my muscles to hold my head up. Now I know to relax and trust the buoyancy of the salt water.

The first three hours are easy. I float and my mind drifts. I imagine the womb must be so much like this. Sometimes I have vague memories of floating inside my mother and the space shrinking until it is too tight and I'm squeezed out. Thoughts of my mother open the door to the demons. Right on time, near the fourth hour, my chest clutches at my breath. What if I can't deliver my ward? What if I'm caught? What if I lose my queen? What if I lose us both? The Commander told me to let the fears come up and build to a climax. "Don't stop the fears when they come up. Stay with them and see them through."

I imagine being caught and held captive. I imagine being tortured to get information out of me. I see my death, or worse my ward's death, at the hands of my captors. I have to squirm and writhe to get through all of the imaginings. The water oscillates under me in sympathy and the salt grows more buoyant as if it's trying to lift me out of the fear. I have eight more hours to go.

After the very long fourth hour, calm returns for the next three and I doze off. When I awake, I am stiff and sore, so I sway gently back and forth in the water like a restless sea creature. The next round of fears arises and I face the terror of never seeing my friends or the Compound again. This fear is scarier than facing my own death. I am back in the moment when I learn about my mother's disappearance. I'm heartbroken once more and I start to weep. I've never cried during a float. I sob and sob until I'm limp, and the water holds me while my tears fall. I picture Alice in Wonderland swimming in a lake of her own tears. I am going on an adventure, like Alice in *Through the Looking Glass*, into an unknown world. Alice swam and swam and kept her head above water. That helps. I will be Alice, keeping my head above water no matter what crazy things happen to me.

Three more hours in and out of fitful sleep and the last hour of the twelve is the most intense of all. It's not that I actually have what I would call fear thoughts. It's that I'm on the verge of losing any hold on my sanity. I can't do anything. I'm paralyzed. Each exhalation goes out so slowly I can't imagine any more breath ever coming in. Each breath is my last. Each one is the last breath of everyone that I love. The last breath of every being I cherish. The end of the Compound. The end of my world.

The lid opens and I am lifted out by strong arms and propped up in a warm shower to clean off the salt. I can't stand on my own, but they tell me this is normal. I'm dressed in a soft gown and laid into bed. Sleep is my best friend. After Hasta.

I awake before the morning alarm each morning. My eyes spring open and I know the bell is ten seconds away. It's the same thing every morning. I count down to myself knowing, without a doubt, that the alarm is following my count. After the alarm sounds, the girls around me moan and stir.

Turning to my side to sit up, the pulse of my wristwatch alerts me that my instructor, Quince, has arrived. I'm to meet her in the classroom beside the float tank. I'm nervous and I put my shirt on backwards and have to take it off and put it on again. Why am I so anxious? The Commander believes I can do this so I need to trust her. She knows my potential better than I do.

Quince is facing a white board at the front of the room when I open the door, and she turns to greet me. She has a wide grin and white-blond bangs that frame her hazel eyes. I'm surprised at how young she is. Is she old enough to be a trainer? Part of me is glad she's near my age, but another part of me is shy and worried. She'll be inside my head examining all my thoughts and she'll know everything about me. Will she think I'm stupid or crazy or both?

"Hi. I'm Quince and you must be Alexa." I squint at her, not understanding, and then I read the page she hands me.

> My name is Alexa Tomson Grant McAllen. My grandmother is Catherine Tomson and she lives in Scotland. I live in New Highlands, North Carolina, and I'm in high school there. I live with a pastor and his wife, Mr. and Mrs. McAllen, who took me in when my parents died in a car accident. We have two Scotties named Brit and Brat. I'm a sophomore and want to go to Appalachian State University when I graduate. I play percussion in the marching band and I love riding my bike and swimming. I've never been to Europe and I've never met my Scottish grandmother, although we've written to each other.

Looking up from the paper with so many questions swirling around in my mind, all I can do is stare at her.

"Alexa is your new identity for this trip. You and I will create a memory overlay made up of the complete details of her life. By the end of our training together, a firm and solid Alexa identity will protect your true memories from detection. I will work with you over the next few weeks to ensure it. We need to cover up all evidence of your life here for your trip. Did your Commander tell you about the Mind Inquisitors?"

I nod. "A little." I'm impressed, and a little intimidated, by her self-assurance.

"I'll tell you more about the Mind Inquisitors later. For now, you should know they are unrelenting in their mission. They are there to prevent any Naturist rebels or their contraband from entering or exiting the country and they will be very interested in a fifteen-year-old traveling alone. It will be imperative that your new identity is strong and unshakable.

"For this trip, your Scottish grandmother, Catherine Tomson, is very ill and nearing death. You are her sole heir and that is the reason for your trip. Trea has planted detailed identification and medical information online for Catherine Tomson, so it will appear when they look her up. As her granddaughter and heir of her estate, you will be issued a Family Health Pass at Port City to go outside of the U.S. Of course, Trea will be sure that all of Alexa's identification papers are in order and planted online.

"The woman in Scotland appearing as your grandmother is really Helen Gravaas, an underground advocate of the Cause and, more importantly, High Commander of the Ward Program. She is acquiring the queen bee for the gardens at the Findhorn Foundation. She knew your mother and can't wait to meet you. She's not actually ill, by the way, but in very good health at ninety." Quince presses a stack of envelopes into my hand.

"Here are a few letters from Alexa's grandmother to give you a feel for the relationship. Memorize them and pack them in your belongings."

When I was little, I heard stories about the Findhorn Foundation. My mom described it as a magical community with sentient gardeners, giant vegetables, luscious plants and insects galore. I don't realize my mind is wandering until Quince taps me on the shoulder. She's not mad, just letting me know how important it is to stay focused.

"You will go through London and on to Scotland. You must always guard any thoughts of your life at the Compound and continuously replay the ones we plant for you about your life in New Highlands. We'll practice until you can stop any and all probes into your true memories. Based on your scores on Mind Command tests, you'll do fine. Any questions?"

Yeah. How the hell am I going to stop my thoughts!?

"Don't worry." Quince answers, easily reading my mind. "We'll work on that. That's what I'm here for. I'll get you ready. There is one solid, unbreakable rule: whatever you do, don't fall asleep when you are with the Mind Inquisitors. Sleep is the easiest state for them to bypass Mind Command and learn your true identity. You'll do fine during the active interrogation and I'll give you a crystalline sleep cap to wear in the hotel. But sleep is your worst enemy during the MI observation. And they will keep you under strict surveillance for twenty-four hours. Twelve hours active testing and examinations followed by twelve hours of mental probing. I can't do anything to protect your sleeping mind when you're with them. I'll supply you with plenty of Alexa material to memorize and reflect on to help you stay awake. JUST DON'T FALL ASLEEP."

Her insistent tone startles me back. She knows I just spaced out again. I nod emphatically and answer her telepathically, "Yes, stay awake."

"That's right, enough for today. We'll start work tomorrow. Study the notes on Alexa's life and get a good night's sleep."

As I leave, I'm not thinking about sleeping, staying awake or my new identity. I'm thinking about what she said to me. "You will go through London."

I've wanted to go to London since I was little and for a very particular reason. My father was thirty-four in 1969 and that's the same year he donated to the sperm bank. He was a famous entomologist and my mother chose his sperm in 2030 over all the other choices as the best one for me, before she even knew who I was going to be. She just knew he was the right father for her child. He was gone long before I was born, but I have a half-brother who lives in London. He's older than me, almost 19. Maybe I can meet him and maybe he will be like my father. I imagine my father to have all the qualities that I know didn't come from my mother. I'm directionally challenged. She is not. I'm an early riser. She is definitely not. I think that my father might have been a directionally-challenged early riser.

For security reasons, I can't put my name on the sibling donor list, a website where donor offspring can ask for information about their siblings. But Hack went looking until she found Abram, who finally last year put his name on the list to communicate with any half-siblings. He posted his request on Christmas Eve, my birthday. Knowing about him was the best birthday-Christmas present that I ever had. Did he somehow know his little sister was born then? I have so many wonderful sisters at the Compound, but I've wanted a brother for a very long time, even before I knew that Abram existed. If he's open to knowing me, I could have a male bond for the very first time and I would love that.

CHAPTER 3

"HOW IS THE TRAINING GOING?" The Commander stops me in the mess hall while I'm clearing plates during kitchen patrol.

"Okay, I think. Commander, can I ask you a question?"

"Yes."

"Did my mother go to Findhorn? Is that where she disappeared?"

The Commander shifts uncomfortably in her seat and won't look at me. Finally, she brings her gaze to meet mine.

"We're not sure what happened to her. She didn't return from her trip to Scotland. We know that she arrived, delivered her ward and left the Foundation, but then we lost track of her. Our guess is that she may be in hiding to protect the Compound. It is possible that you could hear news of her when you're there. Watch your dreams, of course. Signals can come through them and your ward may get signals as well. If your mother is near, she will be trying to communicate with you. In whatever state she's in."

I know the Commander means dead or alive.

"We have so many more tools now to fight the MIs and the political adversaries than we had during your mother's time here. We know so much more now."

I know the Commander is trying to reassure me. But her attempts to calm my fears are making me more nervous. "Was she delivering a queen when she disappeared?"

"Yes."

"Oh." This is a hell of a way to follow in my mother's footsteps. The Commander narrows her eyes and scrutinizes me. She's not a sentient, but my expression must be easy for anyone to read. I know she sees a curious blend of fear and confusion, mixed with a smattering of pride and excitement, spreading across my face. Emotionally vulnerable, I distract myself by balancing a precarious stack of ten plates and back away toward the kitchen. I feel awkward leaving her without offering her my usual hand honoring. The Commander feels my discomfort and gestures to me with her own hands, smiling at my heavy load of plates. I am turning around to go when she stops me.

"One more thing, Gaia. Amey is going to help you arrange for the queen's transport. You can go to her after you finish KP."

"Yes, Commander."

An hour later I hang up my wet apron and jog to Amey's cottage. After bringing me into the world, Amey became my second mother. Gifted with sentience and adept at Mind Command, she taught me how to develop my intuitive gift. After I let myself into her cottage, Amey takes my hand and pulls me down on the floor in front of the couch, tucking me between her knees so she can brush and arrange my hair. She pulls out the band holding my ponytail and the weight of my hair falls onto my shoulders. "I have too much hair."

"You have perfect hair, especially for this trip. It's dark brown mixed with gold, just like your queen. We're going to hide her in your braids. If the authorities ask you to undo them, she knows to duck under to stay hidden. And how to cling to the inside of your clothing too, if she needs to. Don't worry about her. She knows exactly what to do and your job will be to stay calm and unconcerned, no matter how far they go in their search. Trust Rani. Are you understanding her better these days?"

"Yes, I think so. She's not very talkative. Not like Q."

"It'll come. I'm going to make four braids and weave them together for a nest for her. I'll teach you how to do it yourself. She can come out and exercise in the hotel in London. In Findhorn, she'll be free to roam. You're going to love it there."

"Have you been?"

"Yes, I went to the Foundation with your mother on her first trip. It's magical, like the Compound, but even older and more established. You'll meet people there that are like us."

She divides my hair into four pieces and starts to braid. The gentle tug of her braiding pulls up memories of my mom. Tears pile up and I blink fast to catch them before they fall. I miss her. I want her to do my hair.

"I know." Hearing my thoughts, Amey whispers, "She'd be so proud of you. We all are."

I'm too choked up to talk so I send her a message telepathically, "Tell me about her and the Cause. From the beginning." I've heard the story many times, but I want to imagine I'm little and hearing it for the first time.

"Once upon a time, insects were everywhere, free to roam and multiply. They flew and crawled and hopped to their hearts' content and made the world beautiful with their strange sounds, shapes and colors. Some insects put nutrients back into the soil to keep it healthy and some fed the bats and frogs and some pollinated the fruits and flowers and made sweet honey for our tea. Others ate the dead wood to make room for new growth or broke down dead animals to keep bacteria and diseases away from us. They also did sting and bite and sometimes carry other kinds of 'invisible bugs' that made us sick. But we studied them and learned how to heal the illnesses and protect ourselves so we could cohabitate.

"Then the Ext-Pest Corporation came along and told the world that all insects were bad and dangerous and we'd be better off without them. They began exterminating them, species by species, with their chemical sprays and replacing their functions with robotics, artificial intelligence and more chemicals. Slowly, the world's food production began to suffer from the loss of insects and then soon other species, like birds, bats, mice and rats that depended on insects for survival, began to disappear. And it went on down the chain affecting hedgehogs, anteaters, shrews, opossums, armadillos, bats, even wolves, raccoons and bears. But Ext-Pest's profits rose and they became more and more powerful and influential by providing money to politicians who made more laws against insects.

"The Law of Extermination came into being in 2030 and that's when your mother thought of the Compound. She bought this large tract of land with her inheritance and began to collect as many kinds of insects as she could find. Her vision was to build a place where insects could thrive and species could be preserved and protected and where like-minded people could join the Naturist Cause. She built the first cabin here when she was very pregnant with you and that's when I joined. Just in time to catch you when you came tumbling out of your mom!

"Then many more people came to make her vision come alive. We each took charge of different species and began learning everything we could about them. Your father's papers and other scientific studies taught us about the care and feeding of all the insects and, especially, for you and your mom, the bees.

"When she started the Compound, your mother decided that we should keep our children off the grid and away from the outside world. By then the internet was taking over, replacing books and person-to-person conversations, and affecting socializing, community life and education. We kept all of you away from all media, television and computers so you'd keep your own instincts and stay in touch with your deep inner nature. We taught you everything we knew from medicine to literature and math to music. You are the future of the Compound and the future for insect life. You will be here to return them to the world and begin to repair the damage. That's about it. How did I do?"

"You did great. Thank you. I could hear my mom's voice telling me the story."

I reach up and pat my braids and imagine Rani snug in her nest. I won't be alone on this trip because she's coming with me. Amey acknowledges my thoughts by squeezing and rubbing my shoulders. Closing my eyes, I swoon with the pleasure of letting my tight muscles give in to her touch.

"Before you go, I want to remind you about your most valuable resource: your breath. No one can take it from you as long as you live. Your mother taught us this breathing practice. I know she would want you to keep it close at hand. Whenever you need anything—help, support, calm mind, energy—you'll always find it in the space between breaths. In the pause at the top of your inhale and the pause at the bottom of your exhale. The pause holds Now and when you rest there, the present holds you in its embrace.

"Let's try it together. Follow this thought pattern: Breathing in—pause . . . Breathing out—pause . . . Don't worry about the length of the pause. And easy does it, no straining or holding. Just rest in between. That's it, that's good. Remember the pause holds eternity and, in that space, you can do wonderful things with your mind and with the energy around you. You can change the vibration of a room, shift an argument, cure insomnia, or calm a crying baby. The vibration of the pause will create a wave that ripples outward and encourages others to pause in their reactivity. The pause calms your heartbeat, rests your adrenals and balances your chi. The more you practice on your own, the easier it is to access when you need it the most. It becomes second nature. I'm early to bed tonight. Can you stay and practice?"

Amey knows I will. I send her a hug through my mind and she laughs.

"Your etheric hugs always give me goosebumps."

"Come on in, Hasta. It's not that cold!" When my feet hit the water, I stifle a gasp at how cold it really is. But I have to be in the pond and Hasta needs to come with me. My teeth are already chattering and Hasta is not fooled.

"Alright, I'm coming in, but I know it's really cold! And it's starting to rain. Why do we have to do this now? It's a little late in the year for swimming."

I slide down the rock face and splash into the water. Hasta is right behind me and with her hands on my shoulders, she pushes me under. Laughing underwater, I swivel around until we are face-to-face. We wrestle and roll like thrashing alligators before popping back up to the surface.

"You will come back, Gaia."

I flip turn and push off Hasta's thighs, swimming hard and fast away from her. Her words strike the core of my fear. I want to experience everything I love one more time in case I don't come back. Hasta catches up with me and pulls me toward her, holding me close and treading water for our combined weight. She knows me. I know her. We float on our backs and I reach out to catch Hasta's foot as it drifts near me. Now. Now. Now. The raindrops beat a gentle rhythm on my skin. "Hey Hasta! Remember when we watched the rain from underwater?"

"Yeah."

We hold hands and blow out the air in our lungs to sink downward. Looking up, we can see the droplets make little dimples on the surface above us. The reassurance of Now floods my being and we come up together to breathe. Hasta strikes out first to swim across to the other shore and I follow. We swim and swim. The clouds shift and the sun arrives too late to warm us. "Hasta?"

"What?"

"I'm cold."

"Thank goodness!"

"Quince, is this really what goes through a normal girl's mind? It's so boring and meaningless!" I look up from the pages of Alexa's biographic information, looking for sympathy. I am learning about how much a pimple can ruin my day, how I hate PE class and how my feelings were hurt by that boy not looking at me during the pep rally.

"Well, yes. This is all part of the culture and developing a sense of self."

"But doesn't Alexa think about the big things, the things that matter?"

"She hasn't been exposed to them so she doesn't know about them. You have to be shown and taught what matters."

"Why would grownups not teach their children about the environment and the health of the planet and our survival?"

"They have the luxury of denial that you never had. I say luxury because a luxury can be something that makes you more comfortable in the moment, but may not be good for you in the long run. Humans don't like change, especially when combined with uncomfortable conditions. And the facts of climate shift are scary, life-threatening and demand lifestyle changes. Denial is their only escape."

"But that's insanity! It's still going to happen."

"Yes, you're right. It's an illusion of escape, since there is no escape from reality. That's why we need to keep balanced and stay awake to what is really happening."

"Can a few of us make the necessary changes?"

"We'll see. We'll keep trying and see what happens. Denial is just not an option after you're awake."

"Why wouldn't someone want to know? And how are people so unaware? I don't get it."

"It's the hegemony factor."

"What is that?" As soon as I ask her the question, I remember the class where I first heard about it. Last year, our poly sci teacher told us that the hegemony principle caused the disappearance of scientific knowledge and research in 2028. "Wait, I know. Let me try to tell you."

"Go for it."

"It's when one group states over and over again its position until no other position has any room to be recognized. The hegemonic path is normalized and the human species falls in step behind it. Other ideas and beliefs are blocked before they even have a chance to be heard. How's that?"

"That's a good explanation. I'm impressed."

"Ynomegeh is what Hack likes to call it. She spells words backwards when those words become meaningless because of corruption or ignorance. When Hack speaks her backwards language, she sounds like a native of a newly-discovered aboriginal tribe. On the Compound when we are ordered to do something that we feel is outmoded Hack chants 'Ynomegeh!' She always starts it and we join in: 'YNOMEGEH! YNOMEGEH!' It's our chant for change. She wants the elders to listen to our ideas because we may have a better way of doing things. Some of the best innovations have come from our youngest members. Hegemony stifles creativity and change. Technology is ruining everything!"

"Wait a minute. You don't want to become hegemonic yourself. You need to stay open to both technology and Nature and see how they can work together and support each other. If two beings from two different planets were meeting for the first time, they would try to see each other's point of view. Imagine they have never seen your world and you are new to theirs. You would stay open so you could learn from them. And know they're hungry for what you know and what you have lived. Everyone has a hunger for new and wild experiences, whether they admit it or not. You are in touch with the natural world and can help the world remember their true nature. Now back to your equipment."

Quince hands me a soft muslin pouch attached to a belt. I turn it over and minute grains of crystal shift and roll.

"This is your crystalline cap. It doubles as a money belt. When you turn the money belt inside out, it becomes your protective sleep cap. You can let your guard down and sleep without worrying about MIs or sentient spies reading your mind. The outer layer captures and stores any incoming invasive waves. The inner layer holds and protects your unconscious thoughts so no one gets a peek inside that head of yours. In the morning, put the cap in a bag of salt to neutralize the captured thoughts. During the day you'll wear the belt at all times so if anything happens to your luggage you have it for secure sleep. Try it out for a night or two to get used to it and let me know if you have any problems with the fit.

"For your homework, spend as much time as you can imagining your life in New Highlands. You have the descriptions of your friends, home and school. Memorize every detail and replay the new memories over and over again. This will form a barrier around your true memories.

"Here are some more letters from Alexa's grandmother that include details about your mother's childhood in Scotland. Read and reread the letters. They will go far in convincing the authorities that you are Alexa. Remember, Alexa is traveling to Scotland, not Gaia. Alexa will supersede Gaia. Alexa doesn't know who Gaia is. I'll leave you to study and we'll meet this afternoon for Mind Command practice."

I walk to the pond and settle in a patch of sunlight to read. My palms are sweaty from clutching the letters and the pink stationary paper sticks to the worn envelope as I peel the folded letter open.

> My dear Alexa,
>
> I so appreciated your letter about your band concert. I wish I could have been there and I know Mr. and Mrs. McAllen are so proud of you. Your mother would have loved seeing you perform. She was a bit of a ham when she was a wee one and used to make your grandfather and me laugh at every turn. Your photos are so like her. I can't wait until I get to see you and give you a big hug and a kiss.
>
> Lovingly, Gran

Tears are welling up as I read. This is not even real and it's making me cry. Quince would say it's good because it's a sign that I'm already identifying with Alexa. I think it's a sign of how much I miss my mother and want her to make me laugh again. I ask for Now and lie back in the soft grass, bringing my breath into a steady rhythm. Now is where I go whenever I'm upset and my thoughts are bullying me forward or backward. Now is where I feel the best. I need to make Now about learning to be Alexa.

I'm Alexa Tomson Grant McAllen. I live in New Highlands, N.C. Brit and Brat are my dogs and my grandmother is Catherine Tomson. I'm Alexa Tomson Grant McAllen, I live in New Highlands, N.C. and Brit and Brat are my dogs.

CHAPTER 4

AFTER BREAKFAST, THE OTHERS WILL leave for work and I'm to go meet with Quince. It feels strange to know they will go to the fields without me. I miss them already as I watch them pile into the truck. Quince is already in the training room when I arrive.

"You will be interviewed during the twenty-four-hour surveillance. You want to keep Gaia from coming up in your consciousness. They have tricks to slip behind memory overlays. I'll run you through practice interviews so you know what to expect."

"Okay."

"Just do your best and know that you and I will learn more from your mistakes than your successes. Let's begin. What is your name?"

"Alexa Tomson Grant McAllen."

"At your birth, what name did your birth mother give you?"

At the mention of my mother, I lose my mental foothold for a nanosecond and regain it as quickly. "Alexa Tomson Grant."

"Are you sure that is your first given name?"

"Yes."

"Where do you live?"

That one is easy because I have only one address memory. "2241 Eastside Drive, New Highlands, North Carolina 27845."

"Where did you live before the accident?"

"I didn't know the address. I was too little."

"What is your mother's name?"

Once more I feel Gaia rise up at the mention of my mother. I need to work on that. "Which mother? Birth or adopted?"

"Both."

"Sarah Tomson Grant and Mary Stapleton McAllen."

"And your father's?"

Another trigger word. 'Father' brings up bees and Abram. "Marlon William Grant and Terrence Gregory McAllen."

"How long were you Alexa Tomson Grant?"

Another tricky question. I pause and frown. "From when I was born up to my adoption."

"Is there any other name you are known by before you were adopted?"

"No. Well, yes, some of my friends call me Lexi."

"That was good! Your correction gave a feeling of authenticity. We don't want this to sound rehearsed. We need to reprogram two trigger words for you: 'mother' and 'father.' Here's an exercise for you to try. Separate the word 'my' from 'mother.' See the word 'mother' standing alone. Mother is now any woman that takes care of you or nurtures you. Alexa has two. As Gaia, you have many more here at the Compound, but none belong to you. No more my mother, only mothers. Now with the word 'father,' it's different. You don't have true memories of a father. So you have to encapsulate any imaginings of him and keep those safe. Can you find a secure place inside to hold them?"

It's really hard to pull the word 'my' away from 'mother.' It helps me to think that she may have had to pull 'my' away from 'daughter' to keep me safe. Now I need to do it to keep all of us safe. She would want me to do this. When I think about doing it, I cringe with the feeling I get before stripping off a bandage with very strong adhesive. Before I can think anymore, I rip it off. I rip it off so that mother stands alone. And I put all my imagined thoughts of father in a deep corner in my heart. Where no one can go, but me.

I'm lying on a cushioned table under a light blanket with Quince seated beside me. She speaks in a low voice that lulls me into a dreamy state.

"You've made past memories of Alexa's childhood and now you need to create daydreams of what you imagine your future will hold. For example, seeing yourself as a grownup and what you imagine your life might be like. The MIs can almost always detect an imposter identity when they probe for future dreams and there aren't any. We want to make yours very real. So, what would Alexa dream about her future?"

Rich and detailed scenes of my childhood in New Highlands, with my dogs and my adoptive parents, drift through my mind. I start with a visit to my bedroom with the myriad of stuffed animals on the bed and the colorful posters on the walls, then I journey to see my schoolmates and teachers, and finally to my treehouse in the woods. I climb up into my treehouse and settle there trying to imagine my future self. What do I want to be when I grow up? My mind is a blank. All I know as Gaia is the Compound and my duty to protect and nurture the insects. That is the whole of my thoughts and my only wish and goal.

What would I dream about if I lived in the world? A rush of images floods my mind. An exhilarating bike ride on a summer's eve. A first kiss and a bouquet of flowers. Fireworks over a lake. A dinner out with music and wine. A baby bouncing up and down on my knee. Each image in a different setting. Where did I get these ideas? An answer comes telepathically from Quince as soon as I ask. She is helping me with this one because she knows how sheltered I am. No boys and no movies to see how dating and mating are done. I lock down on the images she's giving me and scatter them throughout my cranial space. Is this rush of moving pictures what people in the world see in their minds? After I finish, my Alexa mind is so crowded there is hardly space for Now.

"You'll get used to the fullness in your head. Alexa's past and future memories will settle out and form layers. If you force a yawn now and go toward sleep, you can encourage the layering and, just for tonight, dream as Alexa. Write down everything you remember since tonight you will have a window into Alexa's deep unconscious. Come to me in the morning after you wake up and you can tell me about your dreams. After this, when you sleep, you'll dream as Gaia."

The planted memories tumble over each other and vie for my attention. Pulled between the past and future, I lose Now. How do people in the outside world stand this chaos and confusion? Where am I? Who am I? Where is Now? I'm Alexa Tomson Grant McAllen. I live in New Highlands, North Carolina, with my two dogs, Brit and Brat. That's better. It helps to go back to basics.

Quince lays a second blanket over me and tucks in my feet. As she covers me, I realize my body temperature has been dropping. I try to signal her my gratitude, but I can't move my arms. She lays her hand on my stomach and rocks me gently back and forth and I move from waking chaos to following Alexa into her dream life. It is raw and coarse compared to Gaia's dreamscape, and full of sensations that I have never felt before. A deep pleasure here and a searing pain there. Alexa is of the world, so now I am of the world.

I awake in the early morning hours and make my way back to the barracks to crawl into my bed. What are my future dreams as Gaia? I realize I don't dream of a future. I live in Now and move from moment to moment. For me the future has always only held two realities: threat to the Compound or peaceful Now. And it certainly doesn't help me to replay the possible threats to my world. We do all that in team training, so tonight I'll stick with peaceful Now.

I get to the practice room before Quince and I have to pace to calm my anxiety. I know we need to talk about my dreams, but I have to ask Quince a question first. She arrives, sets down her pack and stares at me, waiting for me to speak. Being a sentient, she already knows what's in my mind but she waits for me to tell her. The tension around me thickens and congeals, tightening my throat. For fear I will stop my own words, I blurt out the question. "How do you know so much about the MIs?"

Quince, who is always quick to answer one of my questions, casts her eyes down and is quiet.

"Quince?" My stomach lurches and I am unsteady on my feet. "Talk to me."

"I was one. I did it for a year until I couldn't stand it anymore. I wasn't sleeping and I couldn't face myself in the mirror. The only solution was to leave."

"How do you leave the MIs? Isn't it for a lifetime? Aren't they looking for you?"

"I taught myself how to reprogram my identity and personality, that and surgery and I am now Quince, at your service. After I knew I was safe, I recruited other defectors to start the MI Underground and we're growing fast. The MIs know we're defecting, but they can't find us, so they can't stop us from supporting the Cause."

I've never seen Quince move outside of her own Mind Command and I catch a glimpse of her vulnerability. She quickly catches me in her head and shuts me out.

"Back to training. You can leave your journal with me and I'll look at Alexa's dreams later. Since you brought up the MIs, let's start there today. When you arrive at the airport, you will most likely be selected for the twenty-four-hour surveillance. We are planning on you to be chosen. To review, for the first twelve hours you will be asked questions about your life: family, friends, activities, dislikes and preferences. You'll also take a written test. I'll explain more about that later. The last twelve hours you will be observed and mentally scanned. Both parts are challenging for different reasons. The first shift, you must watch for and expect sideways entry questioning. The second shift, you must stay alert and awake."

"What is sideways questioning?"

"If I come at your mind from the side, I can get a foothold in any cracks in the memory overlay and get to your true memories. I do that by finding your weak points, where you are most vulnerable. Vulnerability is the dropping of shields and barriers to the true self. Expect them to come at you searching for a sideways entry. We'll practice and I'll find your weak points and help you shore up around any trigger words.

"This is how it's done. I start questioning you about one topic and when we are deep into the details, I will suddenly switch topics to try to catch you off guard. The subject I switch to will be emotionally loaded for you. If you are prepared for a subject change with every question, the sideways entry fails. So, expect them to try it with every question. Stay on guard, especially with emotional topics. Let's give it a go.

"So, Alexa, tell me about your favorite teacher."

As Alexa, I smile and describe the band director, a dark-haired, dreamy man with boundless energy and patience for his students. In the middle of my telling about the school trip to State band finals, Quince interrupts me.

"Your parents died suddenly. How did you deal with that?"

Instantly and without a thought, I'm being held in someone's arms above an open grave at the small Methodist church in New Highlands. I'm sucking my thumb and don't know why I feel so scared.

"That's good. There was no crack at all for me to use. Don't worry so much about your answer to a sideways question. The Inquisitors are looking much deeper. It's your emotional reaction they're interested in.

And you went straight to Alexa's emotions about her parents' death. Let's run a few more to be sure you've got the technique down."

After hours with Quince, I need some time away from Alexa. I can hear her calling me, like a friend that you don't want to see who comes knocking on your door and you hide until she goes away. I feel a little guilty when I do that, which Quince says is a good sign because it means I'm bonding with Alexa.

I slip on my running shoes and jacket and head out for a run. I need to just be Gaia for a while. As Gaia, I wonder what Quince looked like before the surgery and how brave she was to leave her job and how lucky I am to have her as my trainer. Whew, it's good to be back with myself.

I'm with the MIs in a testing room. Bright lights shine in my eyes and I can't see any faces clearly but I know I am surrounded by agents. Then I'm alone, moving unsteadily down a long corridor when a figure appears before me. She looks just like me, except I can see right through her body. She's transparent like a ghost. I reach out to touch her and she flies into me and gets caught in my back. She wrestles with my bones, trying to push me out. I fight with all my might until I faint and fall on the floor.

"Gaia! Gaia, wake up."

"What? Gaia?"

"Gaia! It's okay, it's me, Hasta. You were yelling in your sleep."

I look around me and quickly close my eyes. The room is spinning and I'm soaked with sweat.

"Gaia, are you alright?"

"Brit Brat Brit Brat Brit Brat."

"What are you saying? Gaia?"

"Brit Brat Brit Brat . . ."

The Commander is standing over me. Am I lying down? Faint memories of a girl called Gaia try to rise up and form, then fade away.

Images of Alexa wind around me in a strange dance. I try to reach Gaia, but dogs keep barking and barking.

"Gaia, can you hear me? Do you know who I am?"

The Commander hovers over me, her face large and pinched in worry. As soon as I hear her voice, Gaia pushes forward. Why am I lying down? "Yes, Commander. What can I do for you?" Even to me, my words sound comical. I am obviously not in a position to help anyone.

"Thank Goodness! Gaia, Quince is on her way and she wants to talk to you about what happened. Is that okay?"

"Yes, please." I rise up on one elbow and the room tilts. I sink back into the bed with a searing headache stabbing at my temples. When Quince comes through the door, I start to cry.

"Gaia, first tell me everything you remember."

Sobs keep me from talking for a few moments and Quince's touch on my forehead is tender and soothing. "I think the dream was about a ghost coming into my body and fighting with me from the inside."

"Good, good. Did anything happen in the dream before that?"

"I was with the MIs. There were lots of bright lights. That's all I remember. My head really hurts. What's happening, Quince?"

"I think you went into a mind battle. It's good that we get it treated before you leave."

"What is a mind battle and why didn't I know about it before?"

"It's not a good idea to know all the things that can go wrong with memory overlay. But now that it's happened, we can sort it out. Alexa and Gaia are vying for dominance and both are putting up a good fight. It's perfectly normal for you to want to keep Gaia in charge, but you have to give the power over to Alexa.

"Your dream points to your resistance to let her lead. Alexa needs to be your dominant personality for your trip, at least until you get to the Foundation. Once you're there, you can relax and go back and forth between Alexa and Gaia, but not while you travel. Also, this dream was triggered by fear of surveillance by the MIs. You need to know that you are more powerful and knowing than they are. You need to trust Alexa to get you to Scotland. Can you go back into the dream when you faced the ghost girl?"

I let myself drift back to the corridor in my dream where my ghost-self appears. "Yes, I can see her."

"Freeze the scene there and say to her: 'Alexa, I give you dominance. I trust you are designed to ensure my safety. I let you drive me forward and lead all my actions. I, as Gaia, trust you and give you the reins. I follow you, Alexa, and you alone.' Trust me, you won't lose your Gaia-self in this process."

When I finish repeating Quince's words, my Gaia-self starts to recede, leaving me alone in the infirmary with Alexa. Gaia finds her way to the waterfall and lies on the sun-warmed stone. For Rani's safety and my own, Alexa is my traveling self. I exhale loudly in a sigh of relief and lock gazes with Quince. I can tell that she knows what just happened and that I am going to be okay.

"It's good this happened while you're still here with me. We'll watch for any other mind battles, but I doubt any will occur. You have a strong personality so it isn't easy for you to give up control. But Alexa is also very strong and she can do this mission. She is far more equipped than Gaia because she knows the outside world and Gaia doesn't. Rest now."

In my mind's eye, Brit and Brat run up to jump on my bed and my adoptive mother is downstairs, calling me for dinner. I exhale deeply. I am Alexa Tomson Grant McAllen.

Oh, I hate to toss and turn and that's all I've done since I woke up to pee. It's torture. It's still the middle of the night and I'm so exhausted from the mind battle that I can't fall asleep. I've tried every trick I know including swallowing a gallon of valerian-chamomile-lavender tea. Everyone else is sleeping and I'm so jealous. I can't stand lying here another minute hearing them breathe. I know where I need to go to get some sleep.

The first night we knew my mother was missing, I couldn't sleep that night either. I don't think it had sunk in all the way that she wasn't coming back, but I still knew something very bad had happened. I went to the only place I could go to find comfort. To the llamas.

When my mother started the Compound, she planned for the usual farm animals: horses, goats and cows, chickens, ducks and geese. And then she got a call. An elderly couple living several farms away were moving and had a herd of llamas they couldn't take with them. There were seven adults and three babies. My mother had no idea how to raise llamas and wasn't intending to adopt them, but when she met them, she fell in love and brought them to live on the Compound. Almost all of the original ones are still here and some new crias are born each year. She named the llamas after Dickens's characters: Peggotty, Miss Havisham, Fezziwig, Trotwood, Sydney Carton and Pip. And we keep up her tradition. Two new crias, Ebenezer and Tiny Tim, were born this spring. The llamas are the closest connection I have to my mother. They are a symbol of her love of wildlife and her intention to follow her heart in nurturing and protecting beings that need shelter. No matter how difficult it is or how irrational it may seem.

I was only eight when my mother left. That first night after the news of her disappearance, I dragged my blanket off my bed and made my way to the barn. There was a full moon that night and I remember the tall shadow I cast on the ground under the bright moonlight. As I pushed open the barn door, a reassuring warmth engulfed me. I headed straight to Peggotty, the grandmother of all, and she looked up as if she were expecting me. I dropped my blanket next to her even though I didn't need it. Her soft, thick wool emanated coziness and I nestled into her side. She nuzzled me and my heartbeat matched hers within seconds. A few tears fell, but I didn't know if I was sad or relieved, or both. I slept until Amey found me the next morning. After that, she put me in bed with one of the girls, mostly with Hasta.

Tonight, I need the llamas. I hope Peggotty is expecting me.

CHAPTER 5

I WAKE UP EARLY TO walk in the waist-deep mist floating over the fields, still carrying with me the pungent aroma of llamas. It's time for fall crops to go in and I carry a large bag of seed to the furrowed rows. I wonder if I'll be back in time to see the plants come up. Crows crowd at my feet, stealing some of the seeds as I soon as I can sow them. They know me so well they bump up against my legs. I am recognizable to them as the one who brings them seeds.

I know their cries and can tell when a crow is sending a greeting, a warning or a message for a gathering. I love how curious they are and how they investigate the death of one of their own. They can sense with smell and sight if a death was natural or from foul play. A gathering of crows is called a murder, but not because they are violent or have any urge to kill. I believe it's because they're detectives.

Hack told us stories about how smart crows are and how they can recognize faces. They catalogue the faces that threaten their flock and the ones that are friendly and helpful. She shared an experiment she saw online about scientists, wearing masks, that fed and coddled the crows, while others, wearing different masks, harassed them. The crows learned quickly whom they could trust. This awareness was passed down to the new baby crows by signals and cries. So, years later when researchers put the masks back on and entered the crows' territory, the next generation knew who was a threat.

I hope they remember me when, or if, I come back. I scatter more seeds and the crows pick through them. There is enough for all of them. How did the world forget that when we share, there is enough for everyone? Birds eat their daily portion, trusting there will be more tomorrow. Humans are more like squirrels that store up for the winter, but even squirrels don't take all of the nuts or raid others' stores. Not usually, anyway. Not unless they are very, very stressed. We need to de-stress the world. Or we move into distress. I hope we choose the right one.

My father visited Findhorn! Hack was searching for more information about the Foundation and found evidence that my father was there. She found several articles and a photo of him with the bees. In the picture, my father leans over a hive and a swarm of bees encircle his head. I peer closer trying to see if he's smiling, but I can't make out his face. Soon, I will be walking in his footsteps in the Original Garden. The thought comforts me.

I want to know so many things about my father and his time on Earth. And I want to know what happened to make people in the world turn their backs on Nature. I know he saw it changing when I read his 1970 article about bee extinction. His groundbreaking words were plowed under before they could take root: "What is the self-destructive mechanism at work inside of us? It's so simple—without insects we perish."

Late last night the praying mantis egg cases arrived, so it was Wen that slept in. We will all help her plant the egg cases in just the right places to encourage the babies to hatch. This morning we scooped out the precious cargo of egg cases, each a miniature replica of a beehive. One looked like a tiny coconut and another was already spun tightly around a twig. There will be two hundred baby mantids in each case. We used twine to tie the egg cases in the elbows of branches and shrubs and placed tiny insect cradles in other sheltered spots.

I love to watch them hatch. When the baby mantids emerge, they look like tiny shrimp with eyes too big for their bodies and, within days, they become Zen Buddhist monks in a prayer pose. We need the praying mantises to help balance the populations of other insects in the Compound. Every insect has a duty and an invaluable role to play. I pray that all the insects are safe here with us.

I'm running and I have all the wards with me, some clinging to my clothes and hair and others swirling in a cloud around me. I search for help from the other girls, but there's no one in the Compound but me. I run to the gate and it turns into a huge dragon made out of metal. The dragon opens its mouth and I run inside with all the wards. It shuts its mouth behind us and we are safe there, inside the metal dragon. My heart is racing when I wake up.

Sleep is usually my refuge, but lately my dreams are too real. If I can't escape in sleep, where can I get away? Where can I rest? Find Now. Back to Now. I hear Hasta shifting in her cot. I move out of my bed and slip behind her, cupping my body around hers. She reaches back, takes my hand and draws it up between her breasts. I wiggle closer and she rocks gently back and forth. "Hasta, I'm scared."

"Mmmmm."

"I'm scared to go."

"Mmmmmmmmmmm."

She pulls my hand up to her lips, kisses my fingers and I start to cry. She pulls me closer until we are rocking together and I weep into her back.

The waterfall is my refuge from stress and overload and it's the place I go when I need to be alone with the insects. The rush of water and the ions bounding off the rocks cheer me up. I am glad I'm being sent to deliver Rani and I want to go, but I'm very scared of the outside world. It isn't my world and I don't know the rules. What if I break a rule I don't even know exists?

I lie on a warm slab of granite facing the sky and the spray sprinkles my skin, laying a net of drops on my hair. I wish I could stay here forever and not fight anymore. The rustle of tiny wings turns my head. Two dragonflies dart in and out of the mist and circle me, landing on my arm. They look like tiny fighter planes landing on an airstrip. I am their champion. I have to go for them: the bees, the butterflies and all insects. I must fight for them. My watch chimes alerting me to report to the Commander. I lift my arm up into the air and the dragonflies take off.

"Gaia, I want you to go see Hack. She has some things to show you. You are to go straight into the Telecommunications Room when you arrive at the Command Center."

"Are you sure? I've never been in there. You know my mother was adamant about it."

"I know. This is the one exception. You're going into the outside world and you need to be prepared. Go and meet with her now. She'll explain everything you need to know. Remember to wear your vest."

"Yes, Commander."

I leave the office in a daze. The Command Center has been off-limits for my whole life and now I'm being sent there. The Telecommunications Room happens to be the most dangerous place for me. Since I was very young, I've known that my trigeminal nerve is superpowered making me electrosensitive. I'm like a platypus on steroids and I can detect minute electrical pulses. Sometimes it's a gift, but mostly it's a challenge. When I was small, I couldn't handle lightning storms or being near any electrical source or my brain would go haywire. Thank goodness the Compound runs almost entirely on solar energy.

Hack is the only one of us kids ever allowed in the Command Center. She tells us some of the things she learns from computers about life outside so if we ever leave, we will not be clueless. I suddenly realize that once I enter Hack's realm, I won't ever be the same. The mission feels more real than ever. Halfway to the Center, I remember I have to run back to get my rubber vest for protection. I am glad for the reprieve. I need a little more time with my innocence.

A paper sign hangs on a nail on the outside door and reads: Retnec Dnammoc. It makes me smile to think that Hack made that just for me. She is good at using humor to soften life's harsher truths. She lives in a darker reality than the rest of us and she's always trying to soften the blow when she has to educate us about the outside world.

I take a deep breath and open the door. The lobby is tiny and leads to a second door with another paper signage: Moor Snoitacinummocelet. I'd like to hear Hack pronounce that. The door opens before I can knock. She's expecting me and waves me in with a broad smile of welcome.

Her room is larger than I imagined and she even has a cot in the corner for sleeping. Computers and other strange machines stand at the ready and wires and plugs peek out, curling around each other and connecting to the walls. The electrical current is so strong around me that I have to lean against the door to catch my breath. It is strange to be around so much electricity. Hack holds onto my arm and leads me to a chair near her main computer screen. She has switched it off so I have more breathing room and less fuzz in my cranium.

"So, where to begin? First, you will be outfitted with a watch that looks ordinary, but isn't. It is not connected to the internet so no one can use it to track you, and I have electroinsulated yours to reduce EMF exposure. You will be connected to me and I will not only have your geolocation, but I can listen in on what's happening around you. Don't worry, I'll be discreet!"

I grin at her. She knows that I trust her.

"Keep the watch on at all times. I will send you alerts and you can send an SOS if you need me. The screen has face-to-face and we can also text. I'll use text if an alert is sensitive. If you do get separated from the watch I will know immediately and will check out the situation. You know that I can always find you through the GPS chip in your hip.

"The fourth side button calls me directly and I'll answer 24/7. The rare times I'm not here, someone will be and they will get me right away. Don't hesitate to call me. I'm here for you day or night. Don't be stoic or heroic about getting in touch. You promise?"

I nod.

"It is vital that we stay in touch because it's from here that I can keep you under the radar and safe. I will find any info that you need. Are there any questions?"

"What if I do get separated from my watch?"

"Don't worry about that. Just do your best to stick with it. I'll keep an eye on you and Rani. You'll wear it now until you leave, sleep with it on so you can get used to it."

Hack slips off my old watch, loops the new one over my wrist and fastens it. It's heavier and larger than my old one. I push the fourth side button and I see Hack on the screen.

"See, I'll be right here, right beside you. Even if you just want to talk or say hi."

My heart swells a bit in my chest, filling me with a sense of security. It helps knowing Hack will be a constant techno-guardian for my trip. Next, she takes me over to a seat facing a large, flat computer screen. Her hand moves deftly behind the screen to turn it on. "Now, I want to show you a few sites from the outside world so you can be a little prepared for what's coming. I wish I could show you your whole trip and what it will be like, but I can't. So, I picked out a few highlights. The first is an airport and the second is a shopping mall. A warning, there will be lots of electrical charges coming at you when I turn the computer on."

The screen brightens and miniature people are everywhere, moving quickly in all directions, swerving in and out of each other's paths, with bags rolling beside them. It feels strange to be watching them without their knowledge. The bustle and noise are mixed with a babble of conversations. A loudspeaker announces flights and people swarm, honing in on their gates. It reminds me of a screen of bees, milling about searching for their queen.

With the click of a button, the next scene appears suddenly. Once more the constant clamor mimics the droning of the bees. The multistory building is teeming with people rushing in different directions, carrying bags instead of suitcases. The outside world is not that different from my beehives. I look at Hack and she nods, knowing what I'm thinking.

Another startling thing I notice is the lights, unnaturally bright and stark. Closing my eyes doesn't help because I can still see the luminous imprint on the inside of my eyelids. I am used to daylight, solar-powered light or firelight and I've never adjusted to the intensity of electrical lighting. The computer screen and the lights reflecting off the metal surfaces in the airport and shopping mall are multiplying the electrical charge. How am I going to cope with all that light and noise? Hack reads my mind and turns off the screen.

"You'll have sunglasses that will help with the lighting and headphones for the noise level. You will adjust. It will just take time. I'll give you a balm for your upper lip for your sense of smell, which is so sensitive. But I would recommend that you only use it when you know you are safe because you can learn a lot about your environment from the scents around you. You can smell danger before it reaches you. Any questions?"

The word 'danger' sends a chill racing up my spine. Usually Hack refers to danger as Regnad and claims it is the name of one of her mystical allies. The name has an uplifting and magical ring to it and sounds like a creature that is a mixture of Gandalf and Regalia with regal bearing. Hack says she sports a cape, a crown and, of course, has long silver hair. Thinking of Hack's Regnad takes some of my fear away. An encounter with her is not for the faint of heart. Regnad is to be respected and given a wide berth. That is what Hack says about danger.

My mind is swirling and I can't think of any questions. My nervous system roils, alerting me of an oncoming overwhelm. I need to get out of the Command Center and Hack senses my rising panic.

"You can go. Let me know if any questions come up."

When I am outside the room, I realize that the Now of the Command Center is too intense and unfamiliar for me. I desperately need the Now of Nature. Relieved that I put on my running shoes before meeting with Hack, I strip off my vest, drop it in the lobby and take off straight out the door. I run and run until I can't run anymore. I want the wind I make when I run to blow the images of the outside world off me.

CHAPTER 6

QUINCE IS WAITING FOR ME on the grass outside the Command Center for our next lesson. Sitting in a cluster of clover, she is busy finishing a chain of clover blossoms. When I sit down beside her, she slips the clover chain around my neck and leans back to admire her handiwork. Her gift surprises me and I revel in that feeling until she speaks. "It's almost the new moon and time for you to go. We need to deal with your electrosensitivity. It is your talent and allows you to communicate with the bees, but it's a liability out in the world. On your trip, you'll be exposed to massive amounts of electrical stimuli. You can pack your rubber vest and booties, but you won't have access to them while you're traveling. You've spent your lifetime learning to extend your electroreceptors to communicate with bees and now you need to learn to pull them in."

"Like I do when there's a lightning storm?"

"Yes, exactly. Let's move to the door to be closer to electrical circuits."

We settle on the steps and Quince instructs me to slip off my vest and lean back against the door. I take deep breaths to manage the seepage of electrical current coming through the wood.

"Imagine you are in the airport among the other travelers. Next, find the internal mechanism that alerts your antennae."

When I remember the scenes from the airport, my nerves are automatically alerted and my antennae go up. Quince feels the change in me.

"Ask your trigeminal nerve to contain the antennae for now."

I try to follow her directive and immediately my nervous system refuses. Instead, Regnad appears in my mind which releases more antennae in all directions, making my hair stand on end. "What if I miss something important and Rani is taken? My hypervigilance is my security."

"I know that's what you're used to. Here at the Compound your electroreceptors are protected by the lack of electrical exposure and by your vest. These are superficial fixes. We need to outfit you with a more powerful and unique energetic suit that deflects the intensity of the electrical charges. I'll explain that in a bit.

"Remember, the containment of your receptor antennae is not just to protect you. It's to protect the airplane. Any electrical system that you are near can be negatively affected by you. It's really important that you learn this technique, for your safety and everyone else's on the plane, too."

I could be responsible for bringing the plane down? I had not thought of that and the image brings a lump of dread into my belly. Easily reading my thoughts, Quince smiles. I guess she wouldn't smile if she didn't have confidence in my ability to control my antennae. The lump melts and I turn my attention back to her instructions.

"You need to develop a fail-safe that will let you manage multiple electrical sources without extending your antennae. First, you need a powerful grounding rod to guide your antennae downward. For example, a lightning rod is buried at least eight feet into the ground to ensure maximum lightning protection. If it weren't, the rod would melt on direct contact with a lightning bolt. You need grounding rods as long as your antennae to direct the intensity into the ground."

"But my antennae can go miles and miles."

"So, we need to create grounding rods that go that far as well. To the center of the earth, if necessary. In fact, that's just where we are going."

"How?"

"For you, it's simple. You already have a strong relationship with Mother Earth and now you need to ask her for stability. Well, not counting the occasional earthquake, she is pretty stable. Sit back and start your breathing. Breathe in—pause. Breathe out—pause. Imagine your grounding rods as thick, flexible roots coming from your tailbone and the soles of your feet. These roots naturally seek the center of the earth, snaking downward, deeper and deeper into the earth's crust. Searching for the core. Deeper and deeper. When you reach the center, you have the sensation of an end point, a stopping place. You've gone as far as you can go. How do you imagine the center of the earth? What material is it made of? What color is it? Extend your roots and wrap them around this core. You'll experience a pulling sensation through your pelvis and the soles of your feet. You are secure and anchored."

My roots wind around and around a core of dense blue crystal. A growing sense of gravity draws me deeper into the seat beneath me, yet I am light as air.

"The deeper your roots, the further you can extend your antennae when you need them. And the same roots help you contain the antennae by grounding you and making you feel safe. Now imagine the airport scene."

I am walking amidst a bustling crowd, people jostling me as they move toward their destinations. My nerves are calm and contained. I have Now and can be curious about this strange collective of humans swarming like bees. Quince's voice brings me back.

"You are programming your nerves to know when it is time to release the antennae. They are under your command. The trigeminal nerve is in the sympathetic nervous system and connected to your fight-or-flight system. You can learn to control your fear so the sympathetic system will not go on alert and that way your electroreceptors will be contained. And you'll need a suit with an electromagnetic shield that blocks the waves from affecting you."

"What kind of suit?"

"I have thought about the best design for you. Your Commander told me how much you love the Carlos Castaneda books about the shaman, Don Juan. Your etheric suit will follow his egg-shaped construct of a human light body. Use Mind Command to formulate a transparent and electrical-resistant suit that covers your whole body, like a sheath of transparent gel. The material is from your own design and it will have the ability to deflect the majority of electrical stimuli. You will use this suit on the airplane or whenever you are overwhelmed by electrical stimuli."

I recall Castaneda's description of our bodies as luminous egg-shaped cocoons in his book, *The Power of Silence*. Imagining a construct of super-strength gel that protects me from harmful projections, I install Mind Command to form the suit around me, from top to bottom and back to front. Like an oxygen supply inside a space suit, it's a closed system and my electrical equilibrium is guarded.

Leaving Quince sitting on the steps, I open the Command Center door and go to Hack's room. Hack follows me and stands by the wall, giving me free rein of her space. Remembering to keep my breath steady, I walk up to her lit computer screen and stand as close as I can. My nervous system remains calm. I press my belly up against the screen and still no reaction. From faraway, I can hear my mother sigh with relief. After all the years of caution, I am finally free to explore.

It's four o'clock in the morning and I'm waiting for my ride. Rani is snug in my braids and my backpack is beside me. A swell of sound surrounds me. The frogs and crickets form a riotous chorus. I turn to the watch Hack gave me and activate the voice memo to record the heartfelt send-off. Holding my arm up in the air, I walk slowly in a circle. The moon above is in her dark phase, and even though I can't see her, I sense her keeping me company from afar.

The others are still asleep. Yesterday I cried goodbye to each friend and each ward. My throat is sore and swollen and it's hard to swallow. Where is Jasper? I don't like waiting. Worry thoughts kick my nervous system into high gear and I need to pace to shift it. Fear of the unknown and the anticipation of what's ahead remind me of the night Q left. Rani reads my thoughts and shifts her position within the braid nest to her favorite spot on top of my head. Her soft buzz vibrates my scalp. "Shhhhhhhhhh," she says. She is a mother crooning to her fussy baby. She's telling me it's okay. Reminding me that we have time, we have all the time we need. We are Now.

My panic recedes and I ground in one spot, sending down my roots and swaying back and forth to soothe my heart. Then Jasper's lights appear. The car stops in front of me and Jasper is silent when I climb into the passenger's seat. She gets out to buckle me in even though I know perfectly well how to use a seat belt. I can tell she is nervous and it calms her down to baby me a little.

We don't leave through the gate that I know. There is a back way out of the Compound that I never knew was there. Jasper drives easily and carefully. She is a very trustworthy courier. She always knows exactly where she is going and how to deliver whatever cargo she is given. Today

Rani and I are her cargo. Rani is so calm that I catch her mood even though we are racing along the state road at an incredible speed. I roll down my window and relish the air on my cheeks. I am on the open road and moving toward Port City. I start to stick my head outside the window to let the wind blow the cobwebs out of my mind when Jasper puts a hand on my knee. She is warning me to be careful with Rani. I pull my head in and squeeze her hand. I need to keep my focus. Everything is so new, but I must act as if I know it well. I must pretend that I have always been out in the world.

CHAPTER 7

WHEN WE ARRIVE AT PORT City, Jasper parks the car in front of my airline. She has a worry crease in her forehead and I can hear her thoughts. She's scared for me and reluctant to leave me. I know what she needs to hear and, even though I don't believe it myself, I tell her, "I'll be fine. I'm ready for this."

Jasper nods. Her fear thoughts ease up and her confidence in me pours through my body. She reaches over and squeezes me tightly before I get out and slip on my backpack. I lean into the open window, forcing a grin before I quickly turn to go into the airport. Tears are welling up and I blink them back. I don't want to see her drive away.

Once inside, I am immediately engulfed by a wave of travelers. I let the crowd sweep me along toward security. The lines are long, but move quickly. I copy the person in front of me when I don't know what to do. I see how people move when their thoughts outrace their bodies. They are on automatic, like robots being controlled from an outside source. They are not in Now. Watching them move that way takes me out of my center. I focus on my breath to come back to Now. I breathe in—pause and breathe out—pause, consciously slowing down the world around me. It is fun to watch everyone moving in slow motion as I breathe more and more intentionally.

After getting my passport stamped, I stand in front of the facial recognition camera and stare into the lens. Hack told me to look serious but my thoughts bring a hint of Mona Lisa's subtle smile. Hack has a Naturist Cause contact in TSA facial recognition that can erase any evidence of Alexa Tomson Grant McAllen. With her contact's help, Alexa will never have traveled to Scotland.

My bag is on the belt and next in line to pass through the scanner. The belt stops with my bag in the center and an agent is called over. I'm called out of line and directed to follow the agent who has my bag. I can't tell if I'm a random choice or if there is concern about the contents of my bag. At the end of a second scanner, my bag goes into the hands of a different agent. There is something odd about her. Could this be one of the germanium-based androids that Hack told me might be working in the airport? She's wearing a uniform like the other agents and is attractive with a strong, athletic body, but something's not right about her. When she examines the contents of my bag, some of her movements are jerky and others are too smooth, plus I can't get a read on her thoughts. When I try to tune into her, all I hear is static.

All of us girls learned about GBAs from Hack when she taught us the differences between humans, that are carbon-based entities, and different kinds of androids. Germanium-based androids replaced silicon ones in 2038. Silicon was used first because germanium was rare and too expensive until large deposits were discovered in coal ash and nuclear waste. A very thin layer of germanium makes ultrafast circuits and tiny fiber optics that replicate nerve endings and create a synthetic nervous system complete with emotional reactions and the ability to feel pain and pleasure. Hack told us that the industry boomed with GBAs for hospitality and sex work. She told us to keep that part of the information to ourselves and not share it with our mothers.

Now seeing one, I'm surprised that the agent looks so human. Hack says it won't be long before we won't be able to tell the difference between carbon-based entities and germanium-based androids unless we watch them for hours and see that GBAs never eat. I will know the difference unless GBAs can be programmed with CBE brain-wave patterns. That is, I hope I can always tell the difference. I know that makes me sound GBA-intolerant, but it's only because I love carbon-based entities and am worried about our future.

The android hands me my bag and I smile at her and she smiles back. I feel bad that I judged her, so I telepathically wish her well. I don't know if she understands it, but I am hoping it registers somewhere in her being.

I'm next in line to be scanned. I slip off my shoes and wait my turn. Hack told me to be ready for two different kinds of scanners: millimeter wave machines and X-ray units. She hoped I would get the wave machine since no cell bonds are broken when the waves peer through my clothes and body. She didn't comment on how many cell bonds might be broken if I were X-rayed. Hack reassured me that neither scan would do any long-term damage. I always get queasy when anyone says that to me. Why would you say that unless it was a possibility? But when I think about everything that could go wrong on my journey, the scanner is not my biggest worry.

An agent waves me forward and I stand in front of the dark screen with my arms outstretched. The invisible rays scan me and a tiny zap sparks through my navel. I got the X-ray one. I'm glad I don't have to go through that machine every day. I reground through my feet and hope my cell walls are all still intact. Breathe in—pause. Breathe out—pause. I follow the person in front of me, moving as quickly as I can through the paces.

The last security checkpoint houses the twenty-four-hour MI surveillance. I hand my passport over to an agent and wait with the others in a huddle. As I watch, most passengers get their passports returned and leave the checkpoint. Only a very few passengers are held back from continuing to their gates. Quince was certain that I would be selected and she was right. Jasper had brought me to Port City a day early for that very reason. When they draw me out of the line and take me to surveillance, I just smile and nod.

After they take my bag, store it in a locker and hand me the key, I enter a small medical room with a female agent. An examination table with stirrups stands in the center and takes up most of the room. Quince told me they are not allowed to do an invasive search so I know this is only to intimidate me. I'm calm and composed when the agent asks me to take off all of my clothes. I know that she will also connect me to an oximeter to measure my pulse. She gestures toward my hair, indicating that I should take it down. I know exactly what to do and so does Rani.

I pull out the barrettes holding my braids and shake out the plaits. Rani ducks under my hair and plays hide-and-seek with the agent's fingers as she rifles through my hair. The agent watches me closely as I pull my shirt over my head, shake it out, fold it and place it on the table. Then I continue with the rest of my clothes. I am comfortable being naked since we spend so much time swimming and sunbathing nude on the Compound. My body is strong and I am safely tucked inside. Rani is safe, clinging to my scalp. The guard is watching the monitor for signs of panic or fear. I try to exhibit a little anxiety since I don't want her to think I've prepared for this. I send out just enough anxiety to be believable, but not too much. I know the difference. Quince taught me well.

I am in a small cubicle sitting in an uncomfortable plastic chair and facing a laptop computer. Fluorescent lighting glares down on me while a strong EMF blast hits my face and chest. I've used Mind Command to put on my luminous suit but I still wish that I could wear my vest. I have to keep using a slower and slower breath pattern to manage the intensity.

Questions are popping up and I am supposed to answer them as quickly as I can. Hack showed me some computer basics and I already know how to type, so that is not the challenge. The test is designed to propel me back and forth in the timeline of my life. Quince told me this was to disrupt my connection with Now and make me lose control of Mind Command. I breathe with each question. A question pops up and I breathe in. I answer the question and breathe out. I can keep Now this way.

A Mind Inquisitor disruptor enters my cubicle every ten minutes to interrupt my concentration and throw me off balance. The man who comes in the most often is short and square like a truck. He stands behind me and his breathing is loud and harsh. His electrical signature is chaotic. My chest tightens and I force a deeper breath to focus on Now. I smile because I knew about all of this before coming here. The MIs count on the surprise factor to throw you off and, so far, no surprises for me. They cannot disrupt my connection with Now. Question—breathe in. Answer—breathe out. This test becomes a meditation for me. Thank you, Quince.

After the strip search and computer test, I am taken to the senior MIs. They are sentient and trained in Mind Command. This room is different, set up with comfy chairs, soft lighting and relaxing music, ultimately designed to encourage relaxation and sleep. But I know that sleep is not an option for me. Staying with Now will simulate sleep and keep me on task. My directive is to stay awake.

I go through all the things Alexa has memorized so far in high school: Portia's soliloquy from *The Merchant of Venice*, the periodic table and the history of Western civilization from the Middle Ages up to the present. I review vocabulary for the SAT and I sprinkle it with inane thoughts of how good I'll look in my prom dress and wondering if my best friend Josette still has a crush on our chemistry teacher.

I'm wide-awake. I'm wide-awake. I'm wide-awake. There have already been three MIs observing me. Each taking turns watching me and continuously scanning my thoughts. I keep repeating my mantra. And I wish that I had an uncomfortable plastic chair to keep me from falling asleep. The last MI just started her shift. I have a little over two hours left and, if I pass, they will let me board the plane. Of course, I'll pass. I am Alexa and I'm going to visit my grandmother. I can't wait to see her. I'm so excited to be going to Scotland. I'm wide-awake. I'm wide-awake. I'm wide-

Awake. My muscles jerk as I hastily finish my own mantra. I try desperately to conjure up denial about what just happened. But I know I lapsed. I glance up, trying to look casual, but I'm sure my face shows my distress. The MI is staring at me. She is dark-skinned, beautiful and not much older than I am, maybe still in her teens. She must be good at this, very good to be so young. I try to give my face a mask-like calm. I don't know what will happen next, but she is staring at me and her eyes widen a millimeter. She read my thoughts. She knows.

My vision blurs a bit so I sit very still and shut my eyes, reviewing my storyline. Brit and Brat. Will I get asked to the prom? Will he kiss me? What if I get a pimple? What if my parents don't let me go because I'm only fifteen? I'll convince them, I'll do double chores. I'm so nervous about the AP exams, especially math. The math teacher is so mean. She doesn't explain anything and how does she expect us to know something when she can't even explain it? It's not fair. Brit and Brit. I miss Brit and Brat.

I breathe evenly to keep my heart rate steady. The authorities will check my vitals when the MI alerts them and I'm called in front of the Head Inquisitors. But when I open my eyes, she's reading again. Reading her book and humming softly. She looks up from her book and her left eye twitches in the hint of a wink.

CHAPTER 8

I'M WALKING ON THE MOVING sidewalk toward my gate. Or rather the conveyor belt is taking me there. Moving is so effortless it's as if I've lost weight and gained muscle. I imagine walking on the moon would be like this. I'm sleep deprived and giddy from success. I slip a hand into my bag to reassure myself that my documents are safe and sound, tucked in an inner pocket. I send the young MI goodwill for her whole, long life. I had heard that there are supporters of the Naturist Cause in the most unlikely places. Now I know for sure.

Rani shifts ever so slightly within her braid nest. She is restless, but knows the consequences of discovery. She's been sending me calm since I fell asleep with the MI. She knows how tired I am and how hard I'm trying. She's not upset with me. We are a team and I am grateful for the patience of my ward and the kindness of strangers.

I step off the moving belt and look around me. Electronic screens are everywhere showing people gesturing, talking, arguing, and spouting endless news and ads. Each screen shows a different channel and they seem to be trying to outdo each other. Each screen burns brighter and each announcer shouts louder. I can't understand what they're saying. How do people find Now with all of this audio chaos and EMF interference? I reinforce my strong hold on Now, anchor my roots to the earth's core and beg my antennae to move inward. And with my headphones snuggled over my ears, I hope I won't lose myself in those screaming, flashing screens.

It works and I sigh in relief. But when I reach Now, my adrenaline rush and blood sugar crash at the same instant and I realize how exhausted I am. I remind myself that I can sleep on the plane because MIs aren't allowed on passenger planes. Just a little while longer, I tell myself. I'm so sleep deprived I can taste it. Sleep tastes faintly metallic and a little sweet. It's the best elixir ever. If I have a choice between food and sleep, I'll always pick sleep.

There are more guards at each gate, checking bags again. I try to look sure of myself, like I've traveled before. One guard is a heavyset man with a strong odor. The scent is new to me. I guess it's the smell of male and it burns my nose a little. I want to recoil but stop myself and smile at him instead. He stares at me and I pretend I'm at ease around him, smelling his scent. He doesn't smile back as he finishes looking through my bag and pushes it back toward me. I scoop it up and go to find a seat where I can watch the other passengers so I'll know how to act. I can see my plane out of the window. Just a little more time and I'll be in my seat and I can sleep.

My ears feel pinched so I slip off my headphones. Immediately, the intense chaotic clamor around me rushes through me. I press my ears closed with my hands. I can't believe how much noise there is in the world. It hurts my head and my whole body. It's not only the ambient noise, it's people's thoughts exploding outward from so many crazy, jumbled minds. Thank God for the headphones. Quince was right when she said that the people my age would all have headphones so I could wear mine constantly without worry. I can hear her voice telling me: "Don't stand out. Try not to draw attention to yourself. Be like the others around you. Imitate them and blend in."

Thoughts of Quince and my friends at the Compound remind me that I'm not alone and I slip my headphones back on. I move my hands to my lap and relish the comfort of my fingers slipping in place around each other. With my hands clasped, I study my fingertips. They scanned my fingerprints at security or, at least, they think they scanned them. Quince fitted me with special skin overlays that adhere to each finger. Alexa is now catalogued with computer-generated fingerprints that will disappear forever whenever I choose. Waterproof and durable, they are so thin that I can feel sensation through them. I even have a new fingerprint set and passport if I need a change of identity. Quince thought of everything. I know that I'll have to do my own memory overlay for the new identity, but I can manage. She told me it is easier to hack in and remove facial identity than fingerprints. I don't know why. Maybe it has to do with her contacts.

My stomach rumbles loudly and the sound echoes inside my belly. I'm hungry. Even though I haven't eaten in thirty-six hours, I'm still surprised. My tummy has been so knotted I couldn't think about eating a thing. I search in my bag for one of the plastic cards Quince gave me. I can get anything I want to eat with the card and she will erase any transactions before they are documented. I'm a little dizzy when I rise to stand up and it takes effort to point myself in the right direction.

The storefronts open out on the corridor and people are moving freely in and out. Where are the market guards? I thought there would be guards everywhere. When I step on the pad at the entrance of one shop, a ticket pops out of a machine for me to take. Then I remember what Hack told me about ASD, automated shoplifter deterrent. The pad at the entrance will weigh me and I'll be given a ticket with a bar code registering my weight. At the register, the weight of each item I buy is added to my weight. At the exit, I will scan my receipt and step on the pad. My new weight will be calculated down to the micro-ounce. If there is a discrepancy in my exit weight, after the items I bought are added, an alarm sounds and I am checked for any unpaid items. Hack said that shoplifting is now virtually nonexistent.

Once I collect my ticket, I wander around. There are so many choices. Most everything is packaged in plastic bags or cartons and I can't even tell what some of the choices are. What is Ener-G Goo? It's squishy and unappetizing. What are chips? The bag crunches in my hand, making me think of dried leaves and twigs. Oh, it's made of potatoes. I love potatoes, so I'll try that. An apple. I know that. And salad. And nuts. I'll get these for now. I walk to the lady behind the counter, hand her the card and she smiles at me.

"Do you want a bag, miss?"

I shake my head no and take the card back from her outstretched hand. The person behind me leans around me and sets down a bottle of water and a sandwich. Oh, water. That's right, it comes in plastic bottles. I'll get one of those, too.

After I check out the second time I move toward the door, hoping that I pass through the ASD without trouble. Once through the doorway, I relax a bit. Is this really all I need to do to get food? It's so fast and different from pumping water at the well, picking vegetables, gathering eggs and baking bread. It's easier, but not better. Nothing's better than the Compound.

After shopping, I look around for a place to eat. I'd like to sit on the floor, but the only person sitting on the floor is about three years old and is playing with a toy truck. The teens are off by themselves with their headphones on, either with eyes closed or staring at their screens. I find a seat away from them and open the bag of chips. The first bite is salty and crunchy before my chewing turns the chip into mashed potato. The salt gives me a rush of energy and my brain soaks up the minerals. The crunching relieves some of my stress from the noise and activity all around me. I bite into the apple and am rewarded with a splash of juice. The freshness of the salad is comforting and reminds me of the gardens at home. I open up the water bottle and drink deeply. I'm very thirsty. Water in a bottle tastes like plastic, but quenches my thirst. I put the lid back on and tuck it into my bag remembering what Quince told me.

"Keep track of everything that you touch with your mouth or any other orifice, either flush it or keep it. Your DNA is not on record and we want to keep it that way."

Thinking about flushing my DNA makes me realize I need to pee. Cramming the leftovers into my pack, I find the women's restroom and go into an empty cubicle. I hang my pack on the hook and unbutton my pants. As I'm turning around to face the door, a loud swoosh startles me. The toilet flushes on its own before I can even sit down. I quickly face the toilet and press my back against the stall door and can't help laughing. I'm being intimidated by a toilet. Quince explained a lot to me, but she didn't tell me about loud, flushing toilets. I finish and scoot out of the stall before the flush comes again.

Back at my seat, I pull out my apple and take another bite. The fructose boosts my courage. I'm going to get on that plane very, very soon.

"Miss?"

The strong-smelling guard is standing in front of me and I quickly slip off my headphones and shove my half-eaten apple into my pack. "Yes?"

"Come with me."

My blood thickens and, for a moment, I can't see. I grope for the handles of my bag and follow him. Even from several paces behind him, his scent is strong and acrid. Rani is on alert, still and watchful. I need to act casual, so I try smiling. It feels fake and doesn't help me feel any better. I pass a family eating lunch and I want to slip into the one empty seat beside them and pretend that I am one of them, but I keep walking.

The guard and I are retracing our steps back toward the MI station. Did she tell them? Did my friend, with the beautiful dark skin that reminds me of Hasta, tell them? I follow the guard into an office with two other men. The male odor is even stronger inside the room. But at least they are guards, not MIs.

"Hello. I am Alexa and I'm going to visit my grandmother." Saying it out loud makes me feel stronger.

"Sit down, Miss."

I sit down, fold my hands in my lap and try to look innocent, hoping this is what innocent looks like.

"We are having trouble with your papers. It seems there's a problem with your birthdate. When were you born?"

For an instant, my mind scrambles and I wonder which birthday they mean. Alexa was born on December 12, 2030. Gaia was born on December 24, 2030. I recover instantly to give the only answer to that question. "December 12, 2030."

The two men confer and then look back at the computer screen.

"We don't have any DNA in our records for that date that matches your prints."

"Oh. How could that even happen?"

"Where were you born?"

"In New Highlands, N.C. At the hospital there. I think it's called New Highlands Community Hospital."

"Were there complications in your birth?"

I think I know what's happening and I can hear Quince telling me what to say. I need to act surprised if they bring up the absence of a DNA sample for Alexa. The law of 2028 called for obligatory DNA samples from all recorded births in the U.S. "Yes, I think so. My mother told me it was a very long and complicated labor and they took her by emergency evacuation helicopter to a bigger hospital. I don't know which one."

The three men leave me alone in the room. Will this stop me from traveling? At least I know from Hack that they can't force me to give them a DNA sample. I exhale and try taking a deeper inhalation. Shallow breathing has the advantage of limiting my intake of strong male odor, but the disadvantage of making me light-headed and unfocused. I breathe and rehearse my new identity over and over. Rani is motionless, but I can't tell if she's relaxed or on high alert. I wish I knew her better. I decide she's calm and I join her. It's either that or losing myself completely. I close my eyes, not letting myself compulsively look at the clock on the wall. It's getting very close to the time for takeoff. I can't stand not looking, so I tell myself that I can look again after twenty more deep breaths.

On the fifteenth breath, a new male agent and one of the guards are at the door and the agent walks into the room with a paper in his hand. I paste a smile on my face. He walks over to a desk, stamps the paper and hands it to the guard.

"Take her back to her gate."

I gather up my bag and follow the guard, trying not to show the extent of my relief. For a legal citizen, this might be a normal occurrence, a slight misunderstanding with a simple solution. For an underground emissary carrying contraband, this is harrowing. But I am not an emissary. I am Alexa, a normal citizen, and the mystery of the missing DNA is cleared up. Rani taps two times on my scalp to let me know she's with me. I pretend to scratch my head and tap two times in response.

CHAPTER 9

BACK AT THE WAITING AREA, I take a seat by the window and shift around to get comfortable in the plastic chair. All I can see around me is metal and plastic. I had no idea there was so much plastic in the world. Where did it all come from? And where does it all go after it's served its purpose? We know where wood comes from and where it goes after it serves its purpose. It comes from trees to build and heat our homes and then breaks down to return to the earth to make more wood. What happened to using wood for furniture and buildings? Are there still forests in the outside world?

Plastic: it's clear, white, black, multicolored, shaped and molded and feels cold and aloof. Wood is warm and inviting. I suppose I could imagine that plastic is the new modern clay. But how many of these plastic things were made by hands and not by machines? I lay my arm on the plastic armrest. The resonance wave that comes back to me is slow and hesitating, a vibration with hitches and jerks. Plastic is somewhat real but not quite authentically organic, like a GBA agent posing as a carbon-based entity.

Poor plastic. I feel badly for judging it as inferior and I reach out to it with my thoughts. I get a warmer wavelength back. Plastic is resilient and approachable just like GBAs. Plastic is not so bad but I still prefer wood. With my new thought, the armchair goes cold again and I wonder if I hurt its feelings. I stroke the plastic and it warms to my touch once more. It either doesn't hold a grudge or has a short memory. I wonder which it is?

The loudspeaker interrupts my thoughts and I'm thrust back into the airport. I'm surrounded by my own species, yet loneliness floods me. Something is not right. How strange and troubling and wrong it feels, as if a very important ingredient has been left out of a recipe. I close my eyes and fly to the Compound. The warm sun, the smell of fresh hay, a woodpecker's drumming and a crow's cry greet me and I lift my arms up and breathe in Nature. I am surrounded by a miraculous natural process that humans had nothing to do with. Nature was here before us and she will be here after us. She is cooperative and willing to adapt, but are we?

I return to Now and scan the room around me. Everyone is in their own world, buried deep in their phone or laptop, except for one mother who reads a book to her young son. A comforting and familiar field of energy, humming with warmth, surrounds them. I spot a seat near them and slowly make my way to it. Her voice is soft and made for his ears only and I am touched to be a part of it, even though I wasn't invited. The story is about a squirrel and his adventures in the forest. My whole being drinks in the images and soon, in my own imagination, I am running up the tree branch with the squirrel and my loneliness disperses. We are never alone in Nature. She is always ready to play. Why are we pushing away a favorite playmate? She is forgiving, adaptable and willing to work with us. But she has limits and we are pushing her past them. Time with the squirrel brings my constant plea to mind. "Nature, please give us more time. We are slow and stubborn, but there is good in our hearts. At least, in most of us. Please don't give up on us. Not yet."

Halfway through the next storybook, the call comes over the loud speaker that my flight is boarding. I get in line with the other passengers and there is jostling in back of me so I slip off my pack and hug it close to my chest. I count the beeps as each passenger passes through the last security checkpoint for boarding. When it is my turn, I show the attendant the boarding pass on my watch and she flashes it under the scanner. There is no beep. The attendant peers at my watch, then at her scanner and tries again. Nothing. I try to calm my fluttering heart. I know my watch is not connected to the internet but that Hack has figured a way to put the boarding pass on my phone. Is she sure it will work? The attendant cleans the scanner off with a cloth and sends my watch under a third time. Beep. I send Hack a telepathic apology for doubting her skills.

I slide one foot and then the other down the ramp toward the airplane door. I'm dizzy and don't know if I can bear another obstacle or delay. Rani taps on my scalp again to signal me. "Water. Drink water." I take a sip from the bottle in my bag before I realize Rani spoke to me and in a complete sentence. The joy of hearing her clear message helps me advance down the aisle once I'm inside the plane. The numbers are above the seats and I follow the aisle toward 22C. I'm almost at my seat. It's by the window so I can see out. Hack wanted me by a window because of the clouds. She said they are so thick and fluffy that you can imagine stepping out of the plane and walking on them. I look out trying to imagine being above the clouds, but all I see are men and women in padded headphones and yellow jackets bustling around the plane.

Once seated, I hold my bag in my lap and the weight comforts me. The music playing inside the cabin is soothing, rain mixed with birdsong. I shut my eyes and fumble for my seat belt. I fit it snugly around me and, when it clicks shut, a surge of the unexamined thoughts of those around me spills out like the release of a long-held breath. I had collected all the unsorted and random thoughts gathering in the airport lounge. I don't think the outside world knows about sorting yet.

At the Compound, we are taught to check our thoughts and weed out any projections we put onto others. We hold those projections to sort out later and try to find a balance point in Now to view the person and situation more clearly. We look at those gathered projections before bedtime and use each other as a witness to help with the sorting and to learn more about ourselves. In the airport, projections are flying unchecked out of people's minds. The air is constantly disturbed with these assumptions and false conclusions generating mass irritation and anxiety. I remember Amey's words and search for Now. I can change the energy around me by centering in Now.

Now is hard for me to find and I realize that I expected to feel better once I found my seat. But my body is exhausted from managing all the electrical equipment operating around me. The airplane circuitry is constantly challenging my nervous system, which is already overloaded with human static. This world is bright, loud, chaotic and too much for me. Now feels far away. How are people in the world managing this? Are they managing it or just putting up with it? Do they even know there is another way?

I remind myself that I have a very important job to do right now and I can't afford this thought track. My protective suit is ready, translucent and impenetrable, to contain my antennae for the safety of our flight. I lean back, put my headphones back on, close my eyes and turn on the recording of the Compound. The calls of roosters and dogs, the chirps of crickets, the cries of crows and the stirrings of the wind engulf me.

I open my eyes to a vision of rows of plastic and metal chairs holding a mass of people and I try to bring these two worlds together. I squint and try to imagine all of them on the Compound. It's actually easy. These are people, like me.

Are any of them feeling like a character in *Stranger in a Strange Land*? Do they know what it is to 'grok' something? Are any of them Vonnegut's Bokononists looking for their 'karass'? Do they know the word 'karass'? Am I better for knowing these words? No, not better, because I don't know the words that they like to use to define their existence. I don't know their reference points, but I could learn their language just like I learned Q's. Rani and Q don't speak alike, but are both queens. The chatter is different, but the creature is not.

I smile at a cute boy about my age watching me from across the aisle. He returns my smile and turns away, blushing. That is connection. I feel better. I am not alone here. I'm surrounded by people who will miss the bees.

"Miss. Miss?"

I look up and see the attendant standing over me. The hair on the back of my neck rises up and Rani senses it. "You need to stow your bag."

I clutch it tighter and then remember Quince instructing me to place my bag under the seat in front of me. "Yes, of course."

I tuck my bag under the seat and wrap my arms around myself, hugging tightly. "Almost time to sleep, Rani, almost." I realize I'm talking to myself because Rani has already slipped into her slumber mode. The engines rumble and the lights in the cabin turn off, relieving me of some of the electrical load. Hack made sure my seat wasn't over the engine and that helps too.

I lean my head back, barely noticing the little boy settling in the seat next to me. Curiosity rouses me before I drift off and I glance at him and his mother, who is seated in the aisle seat. She's the reading mother and that makes me very happy. I tuck the blanket around my legs and snuggle the pillow against my chest, imagining for this trip she can be a motherly presence for me, too. I have my headphones, my blanket and pillow and Rani snug in her nest. We start to accelerate and when we lift off, I am pressed back into my seat. A baby cries several rows behind me and makes me think of Amey and the breathing exercise. She said I could use it to calm a crying baby, which I found strange at the time. But maybe it isn't so strange after all. I wonder if I can help.

I imagine the mother and baby as a unit, both stressed. The baby's ears are hurting from the pressure of the ascent. I can feel the pressure, too. Sending goodwill first to connect us, I force a yawn to open my ear canals. As I breathe in and out, with pauses, I can sense the baby imitating my yawn, and growing sleepy. I yawn again and my eyes close. Before I drift off to sleep, the crying stops and I send Amey gratitude. It was just what we needed: the baby, the mother and me.

"We will land in London in 20 minutes. Please be sure that you have all of your belongings and keep your documents handy and ready for security check."

My eyes are glued shut and my mouth is dry. I must have slept the whole way. I peer out the small window to see tiny identical houses and miniature trees far below us. It's like a toy village made out of building blocks. My first thought is that I missed walking on the clouds. I rub my eyes and pull my bag out from under the seat, feeling around for my eye drops and water bottle. The young boy next to me is fidgeting and his mother is gathering their things together. I finally find my eye drops and my grateful eyes soak up the saline. But where is my water bottle? Maybe under my seat? No. When did I last see it? In that office with the men? Did I have it after that? Did I drop it in the waiting area? No, I took a drink on the way to my seat. In a flash of panic, I think of Quince and her DNA warning and my heart clutches. I breathe out and remind myself that no one on the flight knows who I am or is suspicious of me. But then I see Quince again and she's telling me to never let my guard down. Dread gathers its forces and I tap my scalp for Rani. Her "Shhhhhhhhhh" is annoying and does not reassure me.

I turn back to the window to watch us descend into London, the miniature houses growing bigger and bigger. I'm disoriented and my clutching stomach rides high in my body. I know how a plane flies, but it doesn't seem possible now that I am in one. How are we staying up with the weight of so much metal and so many passengers? And with all those bags I saw being loaded into the cargo area? I'm glad I slept through the trip so my brain could avoid trying to comprehend aerodynamics. The landing is sudden but gentle, hardly a bump, and my stomach finds its way back to a resting place. As I'm standing up to gather my things, the little boy dives back under his seat. Without saying a word, he holds out my water bottle.

"Oh! Thank you so much."

He smiles shyly and ducks behind his mother. Quince told me there would be helpers everywhere, sometimes in the most unlikely places.

After Port City, London is easy. Following the young mother and her son, I move through customs and border security without any trouble. When I'm finally outside the terminal, I'm grateful to breathe in fresh air, even with the fumes from city traffic. Any air is better than breathing the air of the Inquisitors.

London feels different than the U.S. The voices and accent are part of it, but mostly it's the relief from projections. The people here seem to be containing more of their projections and there are not as many rogue thoughts floating around. People are more subdued and self-contained than in Port City and I can put my headphones away. I like it here and not just because I'm meeting my brother.

I follow the signs to public transport and find the bus for my hotel. My stomach is filled with butterflies, fluttering with anticipation. After Hack found out where my brother lived, she contacted him and he answered back immediately. He was delighted to hear about a newly discovered half-sister and her trip to London. He wanted me to stay with him, but Quince said it wasn't safe. But she told him he could meet me at the hotel. He agreed and he'll be there when I arrive.

The bus pulls up at the hotel entrance and I find that it's smaller than I imagined. Hack prepared me for a multistoried hotel and I'm relieved that it looks more intimate. In the lobby, there is a young man looking at a rack of books. He has shoulder-length dark hair and is carrying a guitar case. It's Abram. I know it's him. He looks up and knows it's me. Our smiles are mirror images and we walk toward each other, meeting in the middle. When we are face-to-face, I am suddenly shy and awkward. Abram gathers me into his arms and hugs me tightly and I lean into him and start to cry. He stands very still and holds me. I cling to him and never want to let him go.

CHAPTER 10

WE FIND MY ROOM AND I take a long shower, letting the water wash away the tension of the trip. Rani is perched on the towel rack, stretching her wings and enjoying the humidity. Her dish of royal jelly and essential oils is on the counter. She takes sips in between her bouts of flying. I haven't figured out how much to tell Abram about Rani and my trip. I want to tell him everything.

I can hear him strumming his guitar after I turn off the shower. My brother plays the guitar and his music is balm for my ears. I still can't believe he's here with me. After being sure that Rani is content and has everything she needs, I step out into the room and carefully close the bathroom door behind me. Abram has made himself comfortable on one of the queen beds.

"That's beautiful, Abram. How long have you played the guitar?" I feel shy and comfortable with him, all at the same time.

"Since I was seven. It keeps me sane. I think I got my love of music from our dad because my mom can't carry a tune or play anything."

"Was he a musician?"

"I don't know. I like to think so. It was the sixties so I think everybody had a guitar."

"Play me another of your songs." I lie down on the bed near Abram and stretch out. Abram's knee is next to mine and I want to move my leg to touch his, but I hold back. I feel safer than I've felt since leaving the Compound. Maybe I can stay in London with my brother. Maybe together we can find a way to get Rani to Scotland. Maybe my brother can come stay with me there.

The song stops and Abram puts the guitar down beside us. "Are you okay?" He leans closer to me. "I think you stopped breathing."

"I'm okay. My breathing gets really slow when I concentrate. Like the yogis that are buried alive and can survive by slowing down their heart rates."

Abram's eyes widen. "I don't think I've ever met anyone quite like you, sis. You're not of this world."

And I never met anyone like you in my world. You are the first man I've spent any time with. You are my first male friend.

"What are you thinking?"

"How can you tell I was thinking something?"

"You stopped breathing again."

"It's hard to talk about."

"Try. Remember I'm your big brother. I won't judge you."

"You are the first man that I've spent time with or even talked to. We are all women at home. I've only known women."

"That sounds really nice for you. Men are pigs sometimes." Abram grins and squeezes my knee. A shock of electricity sparks and shoots into his hand.

"Whoa! What was that?"

"Oh, I'm so sorry! I forgot I'm supposed to wear my grounding slippers and vest on carpet. I've got a supercharged electrical system and Quince warned me there would be lots of carpet."

"Who is Quince, one of the girls?"

"Uhhm, just a friend. How is your hand?"

Abram shakes his right hand. "It's numb, but I think the feeling's coming back. What do you mean by supercharged electrical system?"

"I'm not sure when my mother discovered my hypersensitivity to electricity. I know that whenever there was a thunderstorm, I would burrow underneath whatever was nearby, frantic to find a place to hide. When she would finally convince me to come out, my hair would be standing straight up. Whenever I would walk by the Command Center, there'd be a loud pop and a yell from inside because I always caused a power surge. All of these things together let her know that she needed to protect me from any negative effects of my electroreception. And maybe that I could develop this ability and use it for good.

"She wanted me to know everything I could possibly learn about electroreception and so when I was a little older, she gave me an assignment to write about it. I wrote a long paper on electrolocation and discovered that bees use it to forage for pollen and that sea turtles, dolphins and platypuses navigate and hunt by it. Well, as soon as I found out about the platypus, I wanted one.

"But my mother told me that it would be cruel to take one from Australia and bring it to the Compound. I understand now what she meant. I also think she wanted me to focus on bees and not get spread too thin. She knew that I had the ability to pick up signals from people, weather and electrical systems so she hoped it would translate to communicating with bees.

"She did everything she could think of to protect me. I think she was afraid that my electrical system would go haywire. She made me rubber boots and a vest for storms and I always wore tennis shoes. She taught me how to send roots down into the ground and how to release the build-up of static electricity. I'm better now and can mostly control it, but I still get nervous when I hear thunder. It affects my whole body, as if every cell, inside and out, stands at attention and sounds an alarm. That's why my mother wanted me to stay away from electricity. She wanted me to have a chance to develop my own natural electro-skills and not be confused by outside electrical sources.

"I don't have the literal antennae to gather a charge like the bee, or use it to hunt in water like the platypus, but my trigeminal nerve is hyperdeveloped and able to send and receive these signals. It's all about electrical signaling using frequency waveform and delay. I don't know exactly how I do it but I can connect with bees and understand their language.

"Since I can sense thoughts and emotions that are carried on pulses of energy my mother knew that I would be able communicate with insects. But she also knew it would be hard for me to be in the world, even in the protected world of the Compound. She wanted me to be able to survive and thrive in any environment so she taught me how to be aware of my breath to control my nervous system."

Abram concentrates on me with his most serious face. I know I'm not supposed to tell anyone about my life, but I'm going to tell him anyway. It's not fair that I've finally found a brother and I can't be honest with him.

"Abram, I need to tell you some things about myself and I won't tell you any specific information that threatens the Compound. So much of my life is a secret, even to me. What I do know is that we're doing important work and that my mother is the one who started it. I not only owe my life to her, but I owe my life's purpose to her. Bees are my life.

"When I was little and would have a tantrum, my mother would call in her queen bee to calm me down. The bee would circle me and gather up my stormy feelings. Bees are very sensitive to energy of all kinds. They can sense a charge, positive or negative, from a distance. You know, that's how they choose a flower that hasn't already been visited by a bee. A bee leaves a certain charge on the flower after every visit. When they are choosing a source of pollen, the tiny hairs on their bodies stand up and give off signals, just like our goosebumps. Every shiver gives them valuable information. I think when we remember our animal instincts we can get just as much information from our shivers."

"How do you know so much even though you were kept away from the world?"

"It's because I've been kept away that I know so much. My mother knew that for me to grow up as sensitive and instinctually smart as the bees, she needed to keep me close to them and away from anything that would stop my natural abilities. None of us were allowed to be around any electronics, to watch television or go on the internet. Our mothers made a pact to keep us away from the media and technology so that our instincts and intuition would stay sharp. Like Mowgli in *The Jungle Book*, we learned to live in the jungle of the Compound."

"So, I guess you don't really miss what you don't know?"

"That's right. And even though I've been sheltered from the outside world, I know history and science and literature. We read all of the time. I understand what it is to be human and to be part of the earth's ecosystem. I definitely know we're not the most important part of it. I don't know much about technology but I'm beginning to see that it's a poor substitute for the abilities we already have inside: the ability to read people and the environment around us and the ability to communicate with other species."

"I know what you mean. Whenever I play music, I know that I'm tapping into a force field that has its own language."

"I'm sure you're right. Music is maybe the closest thing we have in common with other species. Before words, we made sounds and the sounds said everything we needed to communicate. One of the things we have at the Compound is Wordless Days. We can communicate our messages to each other any way we want, except with words. Sounds, music, sculptures, drawings or any kind of gestures like mime, dance or athletics are allowed. It's fun and you'd be surprised how expressive you can be without language and how quickly someone catches on. And if it doesn't work, it's hilarious watching the two of you try."

"I'd like to try that with you someday. Right now, I want to hear as many words as possible about your life. Alexa, I'm so glad you're here."

A tremor of pleasure climbs up my spine and spreads across my scalp. If Rani were on my crown, she would do a waggle dance. The air in the room is misty and thick with connection. I am careful to keep my breath even and regular so Abram doesn't think I'm passing out. I smile at him to reassure him that I am staying conscious. He reaches a hand out to me and I quickly pull in my antennae before his hand lands on my arm. Breathe in—pause. Breathe out—pause. Part of me is floating on the ceiling and my breath brings me back together again. I need to stay grounded and remember my mission. But it's hard not to fly up in the air and laugh and shout.

"Can we go to the swimming pool and play?"

"Yes, my little sister. That's exactly what we're going to do."

CHAPTER 11

AFTER MY SECOND SHOWER OF the day I join Abram on the bed. "Can you stay the night? Do you want to meet my ward? Are you sick of my questions?"

Abram laughs at me in the kindest, big-brotherly way. I wrap my wet hair in a towel and wait for his answer.

"Yes, yes and no. You can ask me questions all night. And I'd love to meet your ward, whatever that is. But what I'd really like is to hear about your home."

How much do I tell him? How much do I hide? How do I do this? I need to tell him about the Compound. I need him to know about the Cause. "We call it the Compound because that's what it is: an enclosed area of land for a particular purpose. Our Compound's purpose is to preserve insect life and continue the art of natural pollination. We live in barracks and have a Commander and we train every day, physically and mentally. That makes it sound sterile, cold and harsh, but it's not.

"There are fields and fields of wildflowers, too many to name or count, and acres of fruit tree orchards—fig and peach, apple and cherry—and greenhouses for avocadoes and almonds, brambles of berries, red and black, strawberry rows and blueberry groves. We grow herbs of all kinds for food and medicine. Our Compound is teeming with life and the amazing, complex wonders of Nature. There are hives of honeybees and flutters of dragonflies and butterflies everywhere and intricate webs woven by our spiders. An army of frogs and a cloud of bats regulate the insects, and snakes regulate the frogs. Each one of us has species that we nurture and guard. They are our wards.

"My best friend Hasta's wards are butterflies, moths and dragonflies. As for me, I'm ward of the queen bee. That was my mother's job before she left and now it's mine. I remember my mother's queen humming while I nursed. I remember the swarm of bees that covered her whenever she meditated by the hive. Her queen rested in the hollow of her throat

73

and the bees covered her until she was wearing a vibrating cape of gold and black. She told me that her meditations were the deepest when the bees swarmed. Their collective hum took her deeper than any chant. She said bees are Om.'"

"Wasn't that scary for you to see as a child?"

"I was never scared of the bees. They're so smart and cooperative, more than humans will ever be. Even when the queen is absent, the other bees work together to keep the hive running. After Q left the Compound, her hive did great. The workers and drones knew exactly what to do. She is a good queen because they follow her orders even when she's not there. You know that our father studied bees?"

Abram nods and I rush ahead. "I've read all his papers so many times and know how smart he was. My favorite paper is about the queen and her habits. I love the part where she gets fed royal jelly. When I was little, I used to sneak into the bee shed and help myself. It tasted like lemon and honey and cumin all mixed together and made me feel strong and powerful like a queen bee. You know that drones and worker bees die after they sting? Not the queen. She can sting and sting and live a long, healthy life. She can defend herself, at least against natural predators. My mother's story begins when an unnatural predator came along.

"Even before the Great Extermination, my mother knew what was coming. She saw it in the push in past decades to use fertilizers, herbicides and insecticides and, especially in 1970, when Ext-Pest put a new insecticide with glyphosate on the open market. Glyphosate started changing plant DNA and threatening insects. The Monarch butterfly was one of the first to show signs of distress. And then it spread to other insect species.

"Next, Ext-Pest invested in research and development for chemical plant fertilization, artificial intelligence and robotic pollination, and the use of glyphosate tripled. The fight against the environmental and human dangers of pesticides and robotics was overwhelmed by greed. Ext-Pest exaggerated the dangers of insects—from Lyme disease to Zika to malaria—to make people get on board. The company tripled in size and began the push for legislation to do away with all insect life. Soon after, it became illegal to propagate or harbor insect life in any form. Laboratories replaced greenhouses, and warehouses replaced fields of flowers and crops. Organic was abolished and replaced with robotic."

I have lived with the gravity of what I'm saying for my whole life, but in telling Abram about Ext-Pest, the overwhelming and tragic losses become more real than ever before. How could anyone destroy Nature for the love of money and power?

"You're doing the not-breathing thing again. It makes me nervous."

"Sorry! I've never had to explain the Compound to anyone before. It sounds so serious and important. Anyway, Ext-Pest stupidly ignores the very important fact that insects pollinate our crops, keep the soil healthy and clean the earth by eating massive amounts of dead material. Also, insects are food for so many species, including us. And they are creative, making honey, wax and silk. And what about their beauty? Have you ever seen a field full of fireflies?"

Abram shakes his head. "Tell me more, Sis."

Sis! I lose my train of thought for a moment, relishing that word. "Okay. Pesticides and fertilizers had already weakened the insect population and with more and more propaganda every year about the dangers of insect-borne diseases, the government decided to accelerate the die-off and started eliminating insect species and replacing their roles with more chemicals and robotics. The fight to preserve and protect insect life was ferocious, but big business won. Little by little, insects were poisoned and their habitats destroyed."

"That is so cat!" Abram's tone is weighted with worry.

"Abram, what does that mean? Cat?"

"Oh, sorry. It means something terrible and destructive. It's short for catastrophic. There were so many catastrophes happening everywhere, I guess we just started abbreviating it. When did this all start?"

"The Great Extermination started in 2030, the year I was born. The same year that harboring insects became illegal, my mother started the Compound. She moved there when she was pregnant with me. She had picked out our father's sperm because of his passion for bees. She had plans for me before I even existed, and she knew that the Compound was the safest place for the insects and for me. She was unstoppable as the most notorious leader of the Naturist Cause. The government, led by Ext-Pest, started worrying about the strength of the rebellion and the importance of her role. After her disappearance, the government thought the fight was over. But the Cause is still going strong in the underground movement."

Although Abram is attentive, my words are not expressing the depth of my passion. I really want him to feel how vital the Compound is to me. How can I show him? Then I remember the audio of the Compound and I press a button on my wrist phone. The room fills with the sounds of my last night at home, cricket chirps blend with frog and cicada croaks and clicks. I turn inward to soak up the pure sound waves and breathe in the familiar vibrations. The waves penetrate my skin and infuse my cells with light. When I open my eyes, I see Abram swaying back and forth as if in a trance. He gets it. I want him to know what I live for. And will die for.

"Abram, how can anyone who hears this, not hear the beauty? Do they really only hear annoying buzzing or a threatening whine of attack? The cicada's hum and the bee's buzz are Mother Nature's free symphony and we are the lucky audience. It infuses the night and serenades our dreams." I turn off the Compound soundtrack and we sit in silence, the room still vibrating with Nature's song.

"Will you let me copy that recording? I want to put it in one of my songs, if it's okay with you."

"That would be amazing!"

Abram's smile quickly turns to consternation. "Why only women on your Compound?"

"It just turned out that way. There were a few men at first, of course, because not all the babies were artificially seeded. But they left the Compound. And then it just turned out, that all the babies born on the Compound were girls."

"This is all so blazar!

"Blazar, like the galactic black hole?"

"That's it. I keep forgetting you don't know our slang. 'Blazar' means amazing and wonderful."

"That is a really good description of the Compound. The only slang we know comes from our moms, and most of that came from their parents. One of my mom's favorite expressions is 'the bee's knees.' You say 'blazar,' she says 'the bee's knees.' Bees hardly have knees at all really, but check out their feet. Those delicate landing pads move around the petals of a flower collecting pollen and nectar, without leaving a trace except a tiny electrical charge. The bee gets what it needs without damaging the flower, leaving the perfume and petals intact. And they have pollen baskets on their hind legs. How cool is that? It's Nature's perfect design, intelligent and cooperative. How intelligent and cooperative are we with our Nature companions? Can we ever learn to be like them?"

"I don't know. I wish we could. Where is your mother now?"

"Nobody knows. She was in Scotland when she disappeared. But I can feel her so strongly. I can hear her talking to me, telling me to stay focused and keep fighting. I don't think I could hear her so well if she were dead."

"You're alone then?"

"I'm not alone. The Compound is my family, sisters and mothers everywhere I turn. But I do miss her."

Abram is at a loss to comfort me and I come to his rescue. "We do lots of different things for entertainment. We read. Novels, research papers, encyclopedias, dictionaries, manuals—anything we can get our hands on. And creativity, everyone has to pick something creative to do each week. It can change each week or stay the same. Hasta, she sings, and Trea writes. I do something different every week and rotate around the different studios, otherwise I get bored."

"One more question. Why are they called your wards? That's not really a word used in America, is it? It's a typically British word, but hardly used here anymore."

"My mother was reading *The Importance of Being Earnest* when she found the land for our Compound. Cecily is Jack's ward in the play, she's an orphan taken in and cared for by a family with means. One thinks of a ward as a person, not a bee or butterfly, but my mother liked the idea of our being the guardians of insects and she adopted the word. She was always looking for ways to hide our purpose."

The ache in my heart swells when I talk about my mother. My chest hurts and I want to think of something else. I want to be in Now. "Do you want to meet my queen?"

"Do I need to bow?"

"No, she's very humble. I'm never sure what she'll do 'cause she has a mind of her own, but she won't hurt you."

"I'm not scared at all."

"Good." I open the bathroom door and Rani lifts off the sink and sails past me. She flies directly to Abram, lands on his head and hums her song of contentment.

"She definitely likes you."

"What do I do?" Only Abram's eyes dare move to look at me.

"Relax. Just be yourself. She's getting to know you."

After we finally turn off the lights, I'm too excited to fall asleep. I lie on my back and listen to Abram breathe. It's different from the girls' breathing in the barracks. It's like a bass, not a flute. I need rest for the trip tomorrow, but I don't want this evening to end. I slip out of bed and stand over him, watching Abram, my brother, sleep. I want Now to last forever.

Abram's hand is curled around mine on the shuttle to the airport. He squeezes my hand and tears rise in my eyes. I miss him already. We have a half-hour ride to the airport, but I wish it were longer. Watching the rush of traffic fly by the window, I realize I'm already adapting to the fast-paced world around me. A pulse draws my attention to my watch and I read: "Stop. Heathrow compromised. Will send further instructions soon. Get to safe place. H."

I give Abram's hand a hard squeeze and point to my watch. He reads, nods, gets up and says something to the bus driver. He stays by the door until the bus stops at the next hotel. I can't feel my legs or arms as I gather my things and follow him off the bus. My heart is rattled because I don't want Abram involved in anything dangerous. And now he is. He takes hold of my shoulders and directs me into the hotel lobby, avoiding facing any cameras. He takes me into the men's restroom and into a stall.

"You need to get to Scotland, right?"

I nod.

"They'll be watching the airlines and trains. So, let's drive. I'll go grab a few things and get my car. They don't know who I am, so they won't be looking for me. And it's more time with you. It's win-win."

Tears well up and overflow. I'm not on my own anymore. I'm going with my brother.

CHAPTER 12

I BUCKLE MYSELF INTO THE front seat. We have ten and a half hours in front of us and it could be longer as far as I'm concerned.

"So, tell me more about your home."

"Well, first of all, I don't know where it's located even though I was born and raised there."

"How is that possible?"

"All of the mothers agreed that it was safer that we didn't know our location. That way if we were ever questioned about the Compound, we couldn't give anything away."

"I understand that part. But if you don't know where you live, how can you find your way back?"

"Hack can find me anywhere. She will find me and bring me home. Without Hack, I can't get home. She is my lifeline."

"So, let me get this straight. You live on a compound, somewhere in America, with girls and women and you protect insects in their natural habitat. And you are the beekeeper."

"Yes. You would love the other girls. I wish you could meet them."

"Me too."

"I already told you that Hasta is the guardian for moths and butterflies, plus dragonflies. She understands them and they love her. You should see her walking around in the summer. She's never without butterflies all around her.

"Sage tends the fireflies, ladybugs, dung beetles, crickets and grasshoppers. Out of all these, the dung beetle is her favorite. You know that it rolls those giant dung balls backwards? And the lucky larvae hatch in an all-you-can-eat buffet. She calls them her diligent workers because they gather up the waste, pack it and take it away. Dung beetles have been running a cleaning service for all of us animals for thirty million years and doing a great job. What would happen to all that waste if dung beetles didn't exist?"

Abram, listening intently, is unable to answer her rhetorical question and can only shrug his shoulders. Not wanting to stem the flow of her story, she rushes ahead.

"Wen looks after all the mantids, one of them is the praying mantis. She's the guardian of those, along with cockroaches and termites. For obvious reasons, her territory is not right next to our living quarters. We would rather have the termites work on fallen trees than on our barracks. We feed scraps to the cockroaches so they can do their job and give nitrogen back to the soil. And cockroaches are valuable for getting rid of dead matter and waste, too. Isn't it strange to think of cockroaches and termites as cousins? Termites are much more social, though. Termites are cockroaches that like to party. And then there's me, the bee warden."

"Whew! I forgot how strong the anti-insect movement is in the U.S. I don't even know what to say. What you're doing is incredible."

"We don't think of it as incredible, it just has to be done." A blush rises up from my neck to my cheeks and I quickly change the subject. "You've always been in a world with robotics and AI. I guess that's normal for you. Hack says that you can buy robotic fireflies on the internet, programmed to flicker and flash. The firefly is Mother Nature's tiny earthbound starlight. It can't be reproduced. Why destroy the original and then spend time, money and energy fabricating a fake one?"

"Yeah, I agree. Some of AI is really weird, like syn-pets. Very real-looking dogs you never have to feed or take out and authentic-looking cats that purr. I don't get it at all. Why have a dog that plays catch or a cat that purrs, but has no heart? Don't we live with dogs and cats to connect with a living being, not a machine? It's Boolean."

"Boolean! I know that one!"

"You do?"

"Yes, Hack told us about it. It came in around two years ago with the WWINFRT: World Wide Initiative of New Facts and Reconstructed Truth, which Hack calls WINDFART.

"George Boole, in the 19th century, stated the two truth values of logic: a fact is either true or false. When WWINFRT became law, Boole's mathematical system of logic was no longer believed because a fact was no longer true or false. Old laws of morality and truth that were the same over centuries suddenly were turned upside down. False facts became truth almost overnight when repeated. False was suddenly accepted as true and true was labeled false. It's all Boolean now. It's bullshit."

"You can use it either way, though. Like using 'bad' or 'wicked' for something really good. 'Boolean' can mean either a solid truth or bullshit."

"That's Boolean!"

"You got it!"

"Naturists hold onto the Boolean logic, hoping it will return one day. So that truth can reset our path to survival."

"I'd love to see old truth come back. It's so confusing this way."

"The chaos is not only confusing us, but actually crippling us. Hack told us that the biophotons in our bodies that emit our radiant health are damaged when exposed to chaos. Chaotic messaging coming from the government causes the body to align with the chaos. Any system in the body can be derailed by chaotic communication between the cells. The human body regulates best with the simple and sane system of Nature. We come from Nature and need to follow her rules to stay healthy, not the rules of an insane and corrupt government ruled by power and greed. Nature has the best plan, if we let her lead."

I reach for the button on my watch and the music of the summer night surrounds us once more. The recording ends and I turn to Abram. "Well, that's says it all." But there is so much more I want to tell him. How do I truly describe the beauty and sacredness of the Compound to someone who lives in the world?

"So why does it sound like a military base when you are anything but military?"

"We use military language for a good reason. There are several bases nearby and my mother thought we could use that to our advantage in case our chatter was overheard. It's part of our camouflage to appear as supporters of the government, rather than rebels. And what about you? I don't know anything about your life."

"It's pretty boring compared to yours. I'm in music school and I teach some private lessons."

"Are you missing classes and lessons for this trip? You should have told me."

"It's okay. My housemate can teach for me. He already knows I'll be gone for a few days and I can make up the classes. Most are performance hours now anyway."

"And your home?"

"I live with Chas. I met him at school and we hit it off. We're more than housemates and and it's serious, he's so gen." Uncertainty arises on Abram's face. "It's okay?"

"Of course, it's fantastic! I haven't been that sheltered. Did you say gen?"

"Short for genuine. And the opposite is syn, for synthetic."

"I guess I'm about as gen as they come."

"That is so true!"

"Tell me more about Chas."

"Chas is sexy and talented and loves me. That's about it." Abram shoots me a grin that says so much more about his relationship.

"He's a lucky guy."

"Enough about me. Get the ukulele out of the backseat and practice the chords I showed you."

I reach into the backseat and scoop up the ukulele. It feels strangely comfortable in my hands. I curve a hand around the body and my other hand stumbles around to recall the chords. Without looking down, my fingers slide into place and I start to strum. I'm surprised it sounds good. How did I get better overnight?

I slowly repeat the three chords he showed me. G-C-D. As it gets easier, I add the strumming pattern for the song he picked out for me. Down-Down-Up-Up-Down-Up. He picked John Denver's song "Leaving on a Jet Plane" for two reasons: it's simple to play and I told him I didn't want to leave on the plane the next day. I think it's a good luck song for me, because I didn't have to take the plane after all. After a few more rounds, I've mastered it. Down-Down-Up-Up-Down-Up. Abram begins to sing along with my strumming.

"My bags are packed. I'm ready to go. I'm standin' here, outside your door. I hate to wake you up to say goodbye. But the dawn is breakin', it's early morn. The taxi's waitin', he's blowin' his horn. Already, I'm so lonesome I could die."

His tenor voice is so tender and alluring that I can't help but join in. I fall into the melody and Abram jumps to a higher harmony.

"So kiss me and smile for me. Tell me that you'll wait for me. Hold me like you'll never let me go. 'Cause I'm leavin' on a jet plane. Don't know when I'll be back again. Oh babe, I hate to go."

I am dumbstruck by how beautifully our voices blend. I didn't know that I could sing so well. After the last note dies away, I can finally speak. "Alright. What just happened?"

"That's sibling harmony. Like the Everly Brothers, the Carpenters, the Beach Boys, and Hanson. They all had it. It's a musical tightness that comes from being from the same gene pool and having the same vocal timbre. And I think we might have it. Now I know that our father was a musician and could sing. I didn't get any musical ability from my mom. She can't carry a tune."

"Mine can't either!" It made me laugh to think about my mother trying to sing. "Do you think our dad knew this song?"

"I'm sure he did. It was No. 1 on the Billboard 100 in 1969."

"That's the same year he donated to the clinic and made you and me possible. This song was imprinted in his DNA, just for this moment."

"Oh, Sis. I love how your mind works, or maybe doesn't work."

Is my brother teasing me? I turn to look at him and Abram's smile almost stretches to each ear. I swat him on his arm playfully. "Can we sing it again? Please?"

"Of course! Let's sing it for Dad."

"Alexa, your leg is bouncing a mile a minute. Are you okay?"

"I'm just antsy. I usually get a lot more exercise than this. I miss Creature Night."

"What in the world is Creature Night?"

"We have it every Saturday. You know how dogs shake their bodies to relieve stress? Well, they're regulating their nervous system. We probably used to do that in the wild, but then lost touch with it. Somebody decided that it looked too crazy to shake off stress so now people just get drunk, have reckless sex and make war instead. I think animals have a much better system."

"What does it look like, this Creature Night?"

"We get together in the Training Hall and we act out any nonhuman creature we choose. And we can change as many times as we want. There's a lot of hissing, growling and buzzing, cawing, screeching, barking and howling. It's a madhouse for fifteen minutes. You can get on all fours and join in or there's a room off the hall where you can curl up like an armadillo or go limp like an opossum. And a few rooms are set aside for anger work where you can be a wild monkey and beat on pillows or scream into them. That depends on the kind of week you've had. The one rule is that there's no aggression toward each other. After that, we all come together for thirty minutes of meditation and centering breath. It's amazing how clear I feel afterwards. And how easy it is to be kind and tolerant after Creature Night."

"We need that in London. Just for managing road rage. Alexa, you have so many good ideas that the world could use."

"The Compound wants to help. We are not the enemy of anyone, not even Ext-Pest. I wish they could see that."

"I guess big business does see you as a threat."

"But we're not! There's money in helping the bees. There's money in saving all the insects. There's money in alternative energy sources. And besides, where are they going to spend all that money if they destroy the world?"

"Yeah, I get it. We could do Creature Night now in the car?"

"Oh, Abram. That's what I need. Ahhh rooooooooooo! Hissssssssssssssssss! Caw Caw Caw Caw!"

Not until I open my eyes, do I remember nodding off with the ukulele resting in my lap. "How long did I sleep?"

"About four hours."

"It feels so good to sleep and not worry about anybody picking my brain."

"What do you mean 'picking your brain'?"

"Oh, nothing. I'm just so happy to be so taken care of. Thank you for that." I stretch my arms over my head and look up at my watch to check for updates from Hack, but there's nothing new from her. With the windows open, the breeze blows the sleepiness off me. I slip off my watch and rub my wrist. "How much longer do we have?"

"About a half an hour."

"I need to pee."

"We need gas, too. I'll stop at the next gas station."

"Rani needs air. If I let her out, can you watch her while I go in?" Adam nods and I slip her out of the pod and open a small vial of royal jelly for her to snack on. Setting it carefully on the armrest between us, I watch her feed. A gas station appears up ahead on the left and Abram turns in and parks.

"I'll wait for you here and watch your queen."

Leaving Abram and Rani behind, I walk toward the station. I feel naked without my watch and even more naked without Rani. Before I open the door to go in, I turn to look at Abram. He's leaning over Rani like an attentive father. It's sweet.

Inside the small store, there's no one at the counter. Abram said the restroom would probably be in the back. There are stacks of water bottles so I'll buy some for us on my way out. Ohhh, it feels so good to walk around and stretch my legs. I open the door marked 'Women' and there's a man inside. Oh! I must have gone in the wrong door. I take a step backwards, my nose burning from his scent. He's too close. Why am I so dizzy? Why is it so dark in here? What is...?

CHAPTER 13

I CLOSE THE CAR DOOR carefully behind me to keep Rani safe inside. I'm nervous about being in charge of her. She's absorbed in eating while I fill the car with gas, check the tire pressure and clean the windshield. I'm getting a little worried about Alexa. Where is she? I don't see her at the counter. I know women's stuff takes longer, but it's been a while. I get back in the car and sit beside Rani, who's still sipping her royal jelly out of a plastic bottle cap. I reach for Alexa's watch and am surprised that it's so much heavier than any wristwatch I've ever had. No wonder she wanted it off for a while. I study the buttons for a moment and put it back on the seat.

I don't like this. Where is she? It's been too long, she should be back by now. Maybe she needs helping buying things since she's so new to this world. I lift up Rani's pod from the seat and hold it out for her so she can slip inside. I place her in my shirt pocket, slide the watch in my jeans pocket and walk to the door of the station.

Inside there's no one's at the checkout or in any of the aisles and so I head to the women's loo, calling for Alexa. As soon as I push open the door, I know something is very wrong. There's a cloth by the door and the strong smell of paint thinner, but no Alexa. When I lean down to pick up the cloth, I feel sick to my stomach. It's got to be chloroform and now I know she's been taken. I rush out of the back exit but the lot behind the store is empty. I run around the building, jump into my car and peel out of the lot.

Where am I going? I slow down to pull over onto the side of the road, my heart hammering in my chest and a hard lump in my throat. I remember Rani and touch my pocket. The queen crawls out of her pod, lifts off into the air and lands on top of my head. I suddenly remember Alexa's watch in my pocket and I reach for it. I have to find her. And I need help.

87

Where am I? Where's Rani . . . and Abram? Ohhhh God, my head hurts. Oh, that man. Rani! Oh, wait, she's safe, she's with Abram. Where's my watch? Did they take my watch? No, no, I left it on the seat. Abram, use the watch. Call Hack.

Okay, okay. I need to clear my head. I am Alexa Tomson . . . I stop myself to scan the room and the house around me for MIs. There are no sentients here so I can be Gaia and use my training. Stay calm. Help is on the way. Breathe in—pause. Breathe out—pause. Slow down reaction time to speed up strategy. Assess. I'm cold and I'm in my underwear. Where are my clothes? Oh, there, in a pile across the room. Was I...? No, my body's okay. My hands are free and my ankle has an electronic cuff that is attached to a radiator. I can hear voices outside thirty yards to the east. Two voices. And Rani is getting closer. I can sense her. Abram, use the phone. Call Hack.

I peer at Alexa's watch.

I don't know how it works. It's confusing with so many buttons and knobs. I close my eyes and try to picture her checking her messages. She touched the screen on the upper left. Please God, don't let it be fingerprint protected! I touch the upper left corner. Nothing happens and my stomach dives down toward my feet.

Okay. Let me try to recreate the moment Alexa received the message in the airport bus. What did she do after the message came through? Did she press a side button to get a keyboard to appear? I press the first button on the side, then the second button and with the third button, the keyboard jumps into view. I quickly type "HELP!" and in several seconds, a young woman's face appears on the screen.

"Alexa?"

"No, it's Abram. I need your help. She's gone. I think someone took her. I have her. . . ward with me."

The young woman speaks to someone in the room and I hear her keying in information. "We have a GPS on her. She's near you on a tract of land about a mile and a half away. Tell us all you know."

"I don't know anything. We were at a gas station and she went inside and didn't come back. I didn't see anyone go in or out. I went in the loo, but it was empty. There was this strong-smelling cloth, which I think was soaked in chloroform. Oh God, what can we do? I don't know what to do!"

"Try not to panic. Alexa's ward is with you, safe and sound? Good. Obviously, Alexa doesn't have her watch with her. And fortunately for us all, she broke a huge rule by taking it off. She does that a lot. This time she broke a rule at just the right time. With her watch, we can stay in touch and I can help you find her and get her out of whatever mess she's gotten herself into. Now, you have to find the GPS bug they planted on her bag. It should be a metal disc about the size of a grain of rice. Feel around the zipper to locate it. When you find it, you will need to cut it out and leave it at the service station. Can you do that?"

"Yes. I have a Swiss Army knife in the glove compartment."

"Good. While you do that, I am going to see what's going on with Alexa."

"Okay. I'll be right back." Rani flies from the top of my head back to her royal jelly. I grab the knife, find the tiny metal GPS and cut it out. I drive back to the station and throw it onto the gravel. "I'm back, Hack."

"We need to make a plan. The ward can help. Have you connected with her?"

"I think so. She flew to the top of my head when I couldn't find Alexa. And then I remembered I had her watch and tried to call you."

"That's good. She's helping you. We need her. Ask her to help Alexa. I'm going to put you on mute for a moment while we get an exact location, so we can guide you to her."

I'm shaking as I reach for Rani, but she is already on my thumb and crawling up my arm. I am very still waiting for her to settle on my head. I whisper to her, "Help Alexa, please!"

Rani hums softly and I wait. Then I know which direction to go. I don't know how I know, but somehow, I do. I know that I should probably wait for Hack's instructions, but I can't sit still. I have to do something. I turn the car around and head back toward London. Driving slowly, I search left and right for a driveway. Rani hums louder and then I see a narrow, gravel road and turn in. I am holding my breath when Alexa's watch speaks to me.

"Breathe, Abram. You are on the right track but I want you to go a different way so you can go into the back of the house. We have an aerial view and can see two people guarding the front and no one in the back. Back out and retrace your route until you see a crossroads. Take a left turn and drive until I tell you to stop."

I follow Hack's directions and, after the left turn, I drive slowly waiting for her signal.

"Stop. Can you see a path or driveway?"

"Yes. I think so. It's pretty overgrown but I think I can get through."

"That's it."

I turn onto the rutted path and drive until the road ends.

"That's great. Turn your car around before you leave it. Here's the situation. You're five hundred yards from the house where there are two men, both in the front. Alexa is shackled by an electronic bracelet, but I should have it disabled by the time you get to her. And I'll work on disabling their van, too."

"How are you doing all of this?"

"Abram, focus. I'll explain later. Go through the back porch and Alexa's in the third room on the right down the hallway. Did you tell Rani to help her?"

"Yes."

"Then we're all set. She knows what to do. You ready?"

I peer at Hack through the screen, waiting for her to tell me something else. I don't know what I want to hear. That it will be okay and that I can do this. I wait with my hand on the door handle.

"You can do this, Abram."

I nod and open the car door. I sprint through the trees toward an old farmhouse and Rani takes flight. I slow way down when I reach the back porch. Cautiously stepping onto the first step, I pause for a creak that might give me away. But there is none. When my hand touches the doorknob, a phone rings and I jump. I hear a man talking on speakerphone.

"Yeah. We got her just in time, before she crossed into Foundation territory. It was a lucky break for us they stopped at that service station. Otherwise, we were going to have to try to run them off the road. We searched her and couldn't find anything."

"Did she drop it already?"

"No, she couldn't have delivered it. We tracked them from the airport."

"Are we sure that she's carrying something?"

"Well, we thought so. Maybe we were wrong. But we have her secure now and will put her on the first flight back to EP HQ. Then you can question her."

"And the driver?"

"What about him?"

"Is he a threat?"

"No, he's just a kid and will probably run scared. I don't think we need to worry about him."

"Remember we want her alive. Don't hurt her. We need what she knows."

"Alright, alright. I've got to go."

"Asshole. He has no idea how hard this is. He should be here, not us. I want to get back home, back to America where I can breathe easy. This is bullshit."

Just a kid and will probably run scared. With that insult spurring me on, I gain courage and ease the door open to enter the house. The hallway is short and unlit and I pass the first two doors. At the third door I stop and try the doorknob. It opens and Alexa grins at me from across the room and mouths the words, "You did it!"

"Are you okay? Did they . . . hurt you?" Abram whispers, kneeling in front of me, touching my shoulders and knees as if to convince himself that I am really here in front of him. "Your clothes?"

I point to the corner of the room. "I'm really okay. They didn't touch me, not that way. I'm sure Hack is already working on disabling this ankle restraint." Abram slips my watch out of his pocket and I clamp it onto my wrist.

"You're right. She said she's trying."

"Grab my clothes. I knew that you would figure out how to call home for me." I whisper into the watch, "Hack? It's me." Hack answers back.

"Hold on, almost there. I already disabled their van."

"Abram, is Rani... ?"

A voice from the front of the house shuts us both up.

"Hey, Jack. You will not believe this. One of the robotics must have gotten out."

"Well, catch it, for God's sake. We'll be blamed for losing it."

"It looks so real."

"It's supposed to, stupid ass."

"How did it get out here from the lab? Was it in the truck?"

"How should I know? I didn't bring it!"

"I didn't say you did." The guard reaches out and clamps two hands around Rani. "Ow! Shit! It stung me!" He flings his hands apart and waves his thumb.

"Don't be ridiculous! They don't sting. You're just imagining it."

"You try! You come catch it!"

"Arghhhh!! Quark!"

"Yeah, serves you right! Now do you believe me?"

"She must have brought it. We've got to get it!"

"You get it! I can't catch the damn thing."

I imagine Rani moving between the guards, easily evading their flailing arms. Back and forth she flies, stinging wherever she can while the guards dodge and swat at her.

"We don't have much time." Abram whispers tensely and clutches my arm.

"Breathe. Hack will come through."

As if willed by the certainty of my words, the restraint releases with a click. Clutching my clothes, I race out the back door into the woods with Abram close behind. The two men are still in the front, arguing about who is the biggest coward, afraid of a little bee.

"Rani, come." In seconds, I feel her alight on my crown. We race through the last of the trees to the car. The car roars to life and we bound over the rutted path, leaving the farmhouse behind.

CHAPTER 14

ABRAM IS SPEEDING, HIS WHITE knuckles curved firmly around the steering wheel. My head is still cloudy, but I feel invigorated. I glance at him again and notice how much paler he looks than when we started nine hours ago. Poor Abram! I've been training for this for my whole life and he just stepped into it. I reach out a hand to rub his shoulder.

"Do you want to talk about it?"

"I guess so. It was like a spy movie. Hack knew exactly what to do. First, she knew about the GPS tracker and told me how to cut it out of your bag and then I just followed her directions. She knew where you were and she was mad that you'd taken off your watch and really glad that you did! The weirdest part of it was that before Hack told me, I knew where they'd taken you. I think Rani knew."

"Yes, Rani will always find me. She's bonded with you, too, Abram, and will keep track of us both. She knows that I feel safe with you, so she'll work to keep us together."

"She flew to the top of my head and I just knew. How did I know that?"

"I think you really wanted to find me and your heart opened so much that Rani could get through to you."

"Hack made me go a back way so I could get to you without the guards knowing. And Rani just took off. Hack said she'd know what to do."

"And she did! She freaked out those guys. By the way, what does 'quark' mean?"

"Oh, yeah. That's what you say when you're really pissed off. Alexa, I want to learn more. I want to get better at this interspecies communication stuff."

"You don't have to learn more, Abram. You've got it. You just have to care so much that the caring breaks through whatever limits you thought you had."

"I hope I don't have to be in a major panic to use it. And I hope I never have to rescue you again."

"That makes two of us." I massage his neck and his guard eases down as his muscles respond to my touch.

"Those photons were talking about taking you to EP Headquarters. I'm guessing that EP is not Environmental Protection, right?"

I'm surprised that he can joke about this already. "Yes, you're right. That's Ext-Pest for you. What did you call those guys? Photons?"

"Yeah, imbeciles, nobodies. What were they talking about anyway when they thought Rani was robotic?"

"Ext-Pest makes robotic insects. They've developed fiber optics so thin they can act as tiny nerves with electrical pulses so the robotic insects can fly and pollinate plants. A very thin layer of germanium can increase mobility and conductivity through nanowires with current-carrying channels and energy-efficient circuits."

"Do you understand what you just said?"

"Not really. Seriously, that's how Hack talks all the time. And she simplifies it for me."

"How did Hack know where you were? Without your watch?"

"I'm not supposed to tell you this, but you might as well know about it. All of us on the Compound have a chip implanted somewhere in our body so we can be tracked if we're taken. The chip is made of a special crystalline substance so it's undetectable and can't be hacked. Hack saw to that!

"Growing up on the Compound is like living in a peaceful war zone. We have to be ready to defend the Compound in an instant and, in the meantime, we're supposed to carry on the work of nurturing and caring for insect life. I feel schizophrenic at times working so hard to be centered in Now and also be ready for whatever might come. We train hard and long. We are peaceful warriors unless you threaten the Cause, and then we're not so peaceful. And it's all to protect the insects. It's all for their survival. But you know, it's really selfish because without them we are lost. They need us, but we need them even more."

"Tell me about Hack. She doesn't sound like a Compound kid. She knows an awful lot about the world."

"Trea was born there, a year after me. Her mother is the Commander now. When Trea was little, maybe around eight years old, she started sneaking off the Compound. She'd explore neighboring fields or just wander around the countryside. Her mother was frantic every time she went missing and tried all sorts of restrictions and punishments, but nothing stopped her. She didn't know what to do with her.

"She got her a dog, hoping that would help protect her, but Trea just left the dog behind. When she was nine, she hid in a delivery truck going to Port City. She found an internet café and that's where her mother found her. She was busily exploring the computer world and knew instinctively how to use the computer as if she'd been doing it for years. She told us later she was so happy to be there. After that, her mother could see that she needed to be in the outside world to develop her talents and she let her go live with Trea's aunt in Port City. She studied and learned everything she could about computers. When she was twelve, she came back to live on the Compound. And convinced the others to put in the Tele Room And that's how we got our very own Hack!"

"How old is she now?"

"She's fourteen."

"She seems so much older than that."

"I think all of us Compound girls seem older than our years, maybe Hack most of all. She's seen a lot of both worlds and has to find a way to navigate between the two. Once we got her all the tech equipment, she found her place and keeps us safe and up to date about the outside. It's hard to remember how we managed before that. Because she was raised on the Compound, Hack has a more objective perspective about the internet. She began to notice that computer data, called New Data, was replacing original data. Originally, data was all the facts collected for future reference and now data is anything that you find on the internet. She says a lot of the internet content is not based on reality and there is very little original fact-based data left that she can trust. Hack calls New Data 'Atad Wen' because she says that it's when a tad of nonsense mixes with a tad of fantasy."

"She really called it. That's exactly what's happening now. It's so hard to sift through the bullshit and get to the truth."

"Hack says 2022 saw the end of age-old truth, now known as Old Truth, and the dawn of New Truth. Hack says that New Truth is designed for cons that take the easy way out and pave their own way to the most advantageous and lucrative path. New Truth is a commodity to buy, sell and trade so the one with the most money gets to name the New Truth of the day. Truth stood solid in one piece before the WW Initiative of New Facts and Reconstructed Truth. Now so-called truth is cobbled together with pieces of lies. With the advent of New Truth, words fly unchecked into Now and statements are fact if written or spoken and sent over the internet. It's Boolean. True and false is no longer true or false. What's important to me is that Nature has always had 'true' hidden in her name."

It's not until I stop talking that I realize what a long speech that was and how mentally and physically worn out I am. Traces of chloroform sting my lungs and my vision blurs when I turn my head too quickly. I'm relieved to see that Abram's hands are relaxed on the wheel and that he's driving more slowly. The landscape eases by the window, gently rolling hills with rows of crops as far as I can see. I smell the sea, briny and fresh. I have never seen a sea or an ocean or even a lake. My leg starts moving again, jostling up and down. We're almost there. The last sign we passed said to take the next right turn.

"Abram, stop up here. Please."

He pulls over onto the side of the road and I jump out to take a narrow path that leads me to the sea flats. Abram unrolls his window and shouts to me. "Alexa, we have to keep going. We won't be safe until we get there."

I feel bad ignoring Abram, but I can't wait any longer. Hack disabled the van and I doubt that other EP agents are close by. Besides that, I have to explore this new terrain. The tide is low, so I'm walking on the floor of the sea. Sunken bowls of standing water, forming miniature oceans, dot the ground. I kneel and stroke a succulent sea plant growing along the side of a shallow tide pool. It invites me to taste it and I snap off a plump leaf. The tang of salt lifts my mood and the saline feeds my blood. It reminds me that I am made of ocean water and am in need of a transfusion.

Abram calls out to me again. He has followed me and is standing by an enormous piece of driftwood rising up out of the mud. It looks like a throne and Abram, beside it with his longish hair blowing in the wind, is the Fisher King. This place looks so different than the Compound, yet it is just the same: raw and wild and still in touch with its Nature.

Rani slips out of her pod to ride on my crown and then takes flight to explore the salt air. "This is your new home, Rani." Instead of her usual "Shhhhhhhhh," Rani buzzes excitedly. It doesn't seem fair that just as I'm getting to know her, I have to leave her. The pain I feel when separated from my insect friends is a different ache than when I am separated from people. Pulling at my ancient roots, the ache warns me that I will truly die without them.

Abram is standing on the seat of the driftwood throne and is calling louder now, his arms waving above his head. He's desperate to deliver us safely to the Foundation. I wave back and walk toward him. I love my brother. He truly is the Fisher King.

Five more miles and we arrive. The houses are modeled after beach-worthy architecture and painted many different bright colors. It could be any other modest settlement of houses, but it's not. It's unique. It's a community started by three rogue spiritual seekers on the site of an abandoned air base. The main street of the Foundation was the runway for fighter planes because the Royal Air Force Kinloss was based here during World War II. After the war it was taken over as a command center to monitor Russian submarines and ships in the Norwegian Sea. I wonder if the community feels the same irony I now feel about standing in a peace-filled ecovillage created atop a historic military zone.

Rani paces on my scalp in anticipation. She lifts off and her buzzing grows louder, and, on her command, I look to my right to see rows of stacked wooden hives. Rani presses against the window in her eagerness. "Just a little longer, my queen." I'm pleased that she is so glad to be here. We drive down the runway road to a small stone house built into a hillock. A goat grazes on the sod roof and bleats either a greeting or a dismissal and then goes on eating. The door opens and a woman moves toward us with outstretched arms.

"Welcome! Come in!"

After a quick tour, we're shown to two rooms with low ceilings and downy beds. I don't know how tired I am until I spot the bed.

"You'll find eggs, bread and cheese in the kitchenette. Are you hungry?"

"Sleep. Sleep is all I need."

Abram is starving and pulls eggs and bread out of the fridge and I collapse against the softness of the duvet. For an instant, I startle up in a panic to get my sleep cap and then I remember where I am. I'm with friends.

It's early and I'm wide-awake, ready to explore. Abram is still asleep and has to go back to London today. I dress quickly and tiptoe out to let him sleep.

Findhorn gardens are so much like the ones at home, teeming with light and vitality that churns out life with the help of the soil and sun. I am touring with the two girls, Tomiko and Julie, who cultivate the vegetables and flowers. I follow them past giant cucumber plants and towering pea vines. A pregnant gourd lies waiting on the ground, fertile with flesh and seeds. Squash vines twist around foot-long fruit. We pass an apple tree laden with fruit. A late summer apple drops at my feet and with the girls' encouragement, I pick it up and take a bite. I can't describe the sensation of the firm give of the skin, the sweet juice on my tongue and the sun-warmed center. Abram needs to visit the gardens before he leaves for London. I'll bring him here after breakfast.

Julie and Tomiko leave me beside the apple tree to start their rounds. I stroke the gnarled trunk and then still my hand to feel the sap rising up from the roots. My own roots are reestablishing themselves after my journey. A branch eases toward me in the wind and I lean back against the sturdy trunk, drinking in the tree's secure nature. I bite the apple again and slowly bend my knees to sink down until I am cradled by the roots. I think I could stay here until winter comes.

"Do you have to go?" I already know his answer, but I cling to Abram like I'm five and he's leaving me with a strange babysitter.

"I'll be in touch. And I can come back and see you."

He looks so guilty that I release him and show him my brave face, to let him know I am not five and that, of course, I understand. "Let Hack know when you get back to London."

"I will. I love you."

His tender words throw me off balance and I reach out to grab his coat to keep from falling. He holds me very close and I breathe in his comforting scent. My face scratches against his wool coat and I want to stay right here forever. After two more breaths, I release him and watch him walk toward his car. A young man approaches him and hands him a paper and keys and walks him to a different vehicle. They spend a few minutes looking inside the car and then Abram settles in the driver's seat. He waves an arm out of the window as he drives through the gate, leaving his own car behind. I miss him already and I'm relieved that it's time to meet Helen, my so-called grandmother, so I can think about something else.

CHAPTER 15

I WAIT IN A LARGE room filled with books, so many books. My hand itches to pull one down and look at it, but I wait. The three founders of the Findhorn Foundation look down at me from portraits on the wall: Dorothy Maclean, Eileen Caddy and Peter Caddy. They look kind and intelligent. An unknown source of guidance brought them to this northern spit of land to work at a hydrotherapy hotel in 1962. They watched the skies for extraterrestrial visitors and spent time in silence listening for guidance to understand their mission.

The inner voices told them where to go after they lost their jobs and lodging at the hotel. Knowing they must not go far, they moved to a sandy plot of land a few miles from the hotel and not far from the sea. Settling nearby in a caravan, they started creating their super fertile garden. From there, they agreed to meet Nature's intelligence with their own knowledge and join forces in the name of growth: inner and outer, physical and spiritual, mental and emotional. They wanted to start an intentional community that brought Nature's spirits in contact with humans. They reached out to try to communicate with the plants and found them answering back.

Their mission was to create a sacred garden in sandy soil and to grow plants that they nurture and care for as they would your own children. People will think they are crazy, but it will make sense to them and that's all that matters. "Dorothy, Eileen and Peter, thank you for listening and following the voices you heard."

Deep in my thoughts, I startle when the door opens and Helen walks in. Slim and athletic, she glides toward me. How can she be ninety years old? Her handshake is firm and transmits trust to me. I know I can talk to her. She is one of us.

"So, you are Alexa." A scintilla of a wink flashes as she says my name. "It's so good to finally meet you."

"And you as well." My speech comes out awkward and formal. Am I supposed to be Gaia with her? Does she know I've already been kidnapped by Ext-Pest? Is she sentient?

"How are you settling in?"

"I love it here. It's so beautiful and peaceful."

"Good. We are grateful that you have come and from so far away."

"The trip was . . . very interesting for me, especially for my first time . . . away from home."

"I can only imagine. Trea told us about the kidnapping. You and Abram handled it so well. We gave Abram one of our cars that never leaves the Foundation, so he won't be followed back to London. Let the kidnapping be a warning for you to stay within our boundaries. You are safest here with us. And I know you want to experience as much as you can while you're here, so explore the grounds and work in any area you'd like. We want you to know firsthand the kind of home your queen will have. And if she's happy here, she can help us birth new queens for other hives."

"Rani." Her name slips out before I can stop myself.

Helen nods. "The Indian-warrior queen. What a perfect name for her!"

Can I share my whole story with her? How much can I tell her? Her sentience registers my concern and she's quick to reassure me. "It is safe here for you and we want you to feel at home."

Relief spills out of me and Helen moves closer to me, taking both of my hands. "We will talk more about your home later. For now, let's have some lunch and then you can explore."

She gestures to the table where sandwiches and tea sit ready for us. She pours a cup, puts in two sugars and a lemon wedge and then hands it to me. I smile at her, taking the perfectly prepared tea. She is a sentient. After handing me the cup, Helen sets a plate of sandwiches on the table in front of me. Then she kneels in front of me and holds my chin in her hands. "You are your mother's daughter."

I blush, transparent under her gaze.

"You know, I can see your father in you as well. Especially in your smile."

"You met my dad?" My mind scrambles to do the math to see if this is even possible.

"Yes, I'll tell you all about it. But first, take a sandwich. You must be famished. I did meet him. I came to camp in Maine in the U.S. and he was one of my teachers. He was the reason I wanted to be a scientist.

"I'll never forget that summer. It was 1965 and I was ten years old and already showing interest in the sciences when my father enrolled me in a camp in the U.S. Your father was the nature guide. He took us out in the field and we each had our own little patch of earth to study for an hour, to watch the life in that square foot of nature. We recorded our findings in a little notebook like real scientists and discussed our findings later around the campfire. I still have my notebook from that summer. After meeting him, I was set on the path to study ecology."

"Tell me more about him. What was he like?"

"He was funny and serious at the same time. And very, very kind. I remember one little boy lost his binoculars and he started to cry. Your father loaned him his very own expensive pair and went to search for the missing ones. I remember, too, that he was musical, but shy about performing. We convinced him to play his guitar one time and his voice was captivating. He sang from his heart. Actually, he did everything from his heart. You are lucky to be his daughter."

Hearing about my father makes me miss him, even though I never knew him.

"I went back the next summer and the next. To watch him with the bees was a wonder! Other beekeepers needed smoke to calm their bees when moving hives or collecting honey, but not your father. He would hum and the bees would rise up and swarm above him letting him lift out the honeycombs. He treated them with respect and the bees felt it. He would be so impressed with your abilities and dedication."

She moves to the window, gazing at the grounds. Should I ask Helen about my mother? She knew her and may have been the last person to see her before her disappearance. But something tells me to wait and let her bring the subject up, at least for now. I'll see how long I can wait. Helen feels far away until she turns toward me, gesturing to the bookshelves. "Would you like to take some books back to your room?"

"Oh, yes! That would be wonderful."

"Take whatever you'd like. Have you taken Rani to meet the hive?"

"Not yet. I was giving her time to adjust." Helen raises one eyebrow, reminding me of Hasta. She knows it's me that needs more time, not Rani. "I'll go tomorrow."

"That would be best. Let's find out if it's a good match."

Helen leaves me alone in the library after lunch. As I roam around the high shelves, so many books call out to my curiosity and my thirst for learning. I pick out a slim volume of verse and try to read, but my mind is elsewhere. I'm worried about introducing Rani to the hive and dealing with either outcome: her being accepted or rejected. I know one of those two things will happen and I don't feel good about either one. If she's accepted, I have to let her go after we've just gotten connected, and if she's rejected, I have no queen bee to offer after traveling so far. I don't want to wait until tomorrow. I'm not good at not knowing and I'm not good at waiting.

Leaving the books behind, I rush past greenhouses of tomatoes and herbs and weave in and out of rows of zucchini the size of pumpkins and cucumbers the size of gourds. I hear the hives before I spot the colorful boxes stacked atop each other in a circle. In the center of the boxes there's a hooded figure in white pants and tunic. The slow motion and delicate flicker of fingers and wrists evoke the flight of bees. The movements are deliberate and graceful, like Tai Chi and Qigong, but the configurations are strange to me. A sacred air surrounds the figure, so I stay very still not wanting to disturb the dance. Wisps of luminescence trail out of the dancer's fingertips. The light streams hang in midair and when I blink, they reappear on the back of my eyelids. Is it my imagination or a trick of the light or is the dancer bioluminescent?

As I back away, I admit to myself that I'm glad today isn't the day. Rani and I will come tomorrow and hope to meet the keeper. With Rani still atop my head, I hasten back toward the greenhouses. Rani starts to chatter, the same strange chatter she spoke the first night we met. But this time I understand her. She's asking me "Why?" I need to explain to her what I'm feeling and hope she understands.

"I can't leave you yet. Once I turn you over to your new hive, I won't have a purpose. And I've never been without a purpose. It has always been caring for bees, training with my team and protecting the Compound. At least as long as I keep you with me, I still have a purpose." I wait for Rani to answer me with her usual "Shhhhhhhhhh." She is silent as she flies to alight on my hand. I raise her up until we are staring at one another. I wait, tilting my head to one side. Rani tilts her head and mirrors me, and lifts off to land on my watch. Just as she lands, her fuzzy body is backlit on the watch face by a text alert from Hack.

"I just got this from Abram via email: 'I need Alexa. Can she come to the driftwood?' Do you understand his message?"

"Yes. Tell him yes. I'll meet him there. Did he say anything else?"

"No, that's all."

"Thanks, Hack. I'll go right now."

My stomach churns as I disconnect. Rani lifts off my watch and flies to my crown. Abram should be on his way to London.

The wind tugs at my jacket and I draw it tighter around me. I watch my feet trace smaller and smaller circles around the scattered pools of water. I breathe in the briny air and try to stay grounded. Rani is tucked inside a braid and on alert.

I hear Abram's car arrive and park. I stand taller, searching for him on the horizon, when I see three figures appear. Abram is in the middle, dwarfed by the two women flanking him. He walks mechanically and his face is pinched with concern. They are not touching him, but he seems locked between them. I feel angry that Abram's once more in a difficult position because of me. Cautionary prickles ripple up my neck and Rani anchors her feet more securely as the goosebumps reach my scalp. I stride toward them, unafraid, yet completely on guard.

"What's going on?"

I scan the tall, athletic women on either side of Abram. My brain knows what I see but does not accept it. Identical faces with identical dark circles under identical liquid brown eyes. Strong chins and sculpted cheeks. Twins. Young, foreign and powerful. I quickly scan the two minds in front of me and bump into an unfamiliar form of Mind Command. They remind me of someone. I know them. I don't know how I know them, but I do.

"I'm waiting." I don't know what else to say. My mind searches through files. Why are they so familiar to me? Finally, I can't stand the silence any longer. "Abram, are you okay?"

"Yes."

"Why are you here?" Out of patience, my tone is harsh.

"We do not want to hurt you." The accent is Russian.

"Okay." I am slightly relieved, but still wary.

"We have been camping outside of the Foundation for days, trying to find a way in. We know you have to be invited and we don't have any contacts to allow this. We are from Russia and that seems to work against us at every turn. My name is Dania and I am an apiarist, and my sister, Svetlana, is an aurelian."

Bees and butterflies? Why, they are just like me and Hasta!

"Alexa, they were on their way to Findhorn and had car trouble, so I gave them a ride." Abram's voice is tentative. The two women look down at their feet, visibly uncomfortable. The hairs rise on my neck and won't let down. If I were a dog, would they hear a low, threatening growl? Svetlana moves backwards one step before speaking.

"When your brother stopped to check on us and told us he was visiting his sister, we asked if he would escort us here. We could not believe the luck of finding the brother of a beekeeper."

Dania steps forward past her sister.

"We need your help and your brother was kind enough to stop and listen to our story when we flagged him down. We are grateful that he trusted us enough to bring us to meet you. Please, do not be angry. We want to learn all we can from the people here and take it back to our gardens in Vladivostok. We are desperate to help our bees and butterflies."

My primitive hackles dwindle and recede and Rani settles down with them. There is truth reflected in their voices. I know the markings of a screen identity and there are none. They are who they say they are. If their story hadn't convinced me, the shadows under their eyes would have. I turn my attention back to Abram and realize the source of his anxiety is not about the two women, but rather how I am taking this unplanned meeting.

"Abram, come here." I take his arm and link it with mine. "You did right to bring them to me."

His relief is so obvious that I can't help but laugh. The twins sense my laughter as a sign of acceptance and join me with soft chuckles. The laughing contagion is complete when Abram catches it. Even while I'm laughing, the seriousness of the situation returns to me and I remind myself that I need to be Alexa when I'm around the twins. Even though they are gen, I must stay cautious and protective. "You two wait here while I go to the Foundation to get permission for you to visit. I'll come back for you. And please, leave Abram out of this from now on." My voice is strong and unyielding.

"We only asked him because we thought we might have a chance to meet with you. We did not mean any harm."

"Well, he didn't know that." I turn to Abram and shrug my shoulders. He shrugs back at me and reaches out to hug me. "You had no idea that a little sister would bring so much drama into your life, did you?"

He takes my shoulders and looks deep into my eyes, as if to ask me, "Do you trust them?" I know he will trust them if I do. I nod my head, but he steps closer and whispers, "I don't want to leave you."

"I'll be okay, trust me. You need to get back to London. And I'm so sorry for all this."

Abram shakes his head to dismiss my apology. "You're family. No amount of drama is too much for me to put up with. Except maybe another kidnapping." He gives my cheek a quick kiss.

"Go. I'm alright, I promise."

The women are silent as we all three walk Abram to the car. After he drives away, I turn toward my two new students and reach out my hand. I will be Alexa with them, but teach them from Gaia's knowledge. "I do understand. Desperation makes us all cross lines."

CHAPTER 16

"HACK, CAN YOU FIND OUT all you can about Svetlana and Dania? Helen wants them to be able to stay and I want to be sure they are not a threat."

"I've heard of them from others in the Cause. I think they're legit but I'll do a more thorough search. But the most important thing is what you feel. What does your radar say about them? Do you trust them?"

"They aren't here to do any harm. They want me to train them. But I don't know how I do what I do. I just do it. I don't think I can teach it."

"The insects trust you because your heart is pure. That's how you do it, with your heart."

"Maybe I could teach someone with a pure heart, someone like Hasta. But I'm not sure about them yet."

"Give yourself some time to get to know them better."

"I will. So, tell me, what's happening at home?"

"There was drama around the katydid delivery." Hack's face flushes and her tangled curly hair stands out like a halo. "The truck had a flat tire and the driver was really scared about being discovered. It turns out a very nice cop helped her fix the tire and sent her on her way with no inspection. Luck or a supporter of the Cause? Who knows?"

"How is Sage doing with all this?"

"A little rattled right after, and now rushing around finding the best sites for the cocoons. She sends her love and wishes you were here. No one can climb as high as you can. Remember when we settled two hundred cocoons in one night?"

A swell of homesickness surprises me and swallows my breath. I open my mouth to answer her and nothing comes out.

"Are you there?"

"Yeah, sorry. Just got distracted by something here. I've gotta go. I miss you all." I rush to disconnect before she can respond. I have never hung up first when talking to Hack, until tonight. Admitting how much

I miss them makes my head pound and the room spin. Can I hitchhike to London? Does Findhorn have llamas?

Today's the day to meet the Findhorn beekeeper. No more putting it off. I take a run with Rani before we head to the bee yard and she tells me several things during my cooldown.

First, she is with me always, whether I sense her or not. Second, she wants to be right here, where she always is, in Now. And lastly, I want to be right here, where I am, whether I can admit it or not. She knows that I am more nervous than she is about her new guardian. She's telling me to trust whoever it is to take good care of her.

I arrive at the bee yard and spy the beekeeper hovering over a hive, still in white and with no protective gear. As I get closer, the figure turns and flashes the grin of a gentle trickster. The youthful dancer that I saw was Helen. She is so adept at masking that I couldn't detect this part of her life.

"You got me, Helen." A sweet mixture of surprise and delight floods my senses, a rare sensation for sentients. Sentients so often know what's coming ahead of time that it's rare to be surprised. I walk up to her and hold out my cupped hands. She does the same and we bow to each other. An effervescent air surrounds our solemnity.

"What was that dance you were doing by the hives yesterday?"

"It is called Kutai and comes from the Indonesian island of Borneo. The movements are a mix of Balinese and Japanese sacred dances and martial arts. I do a ritual dance before I tend the bees. The one you saw is the Dance of All Winged Creatures."

"Can you teach me?"

"Of course. Anytime you'd like."

Her sincere invitation should lift my spirits but all I feel is an acute sense of loss. Once Rani is settled, my quest will end. No more words are spoken between us as we approach the hives. We both know that there is a chance that Rani will be rejected and I will have risked coming the long distance for nothing. I feel afraid and oddly responsible for the possibility of failure, even though I have no control over it. I wonder if Helen feels the same.

Helen hums over the hives. Did my father teach her to do that? The bees are tranquil as she pulls out a frame. I hold Rani in her small safety cage up near my heart. When a hive is unhappy with a new queen, they surround the cage and hunch over the queen, preparing to sting her to death. The cage is Rani's protection so we can rescue her if this happens. We have to accept whatever happens. Nature is taking her course.

I hold my breath and set the cage on top of the frame. The bees immediately draw close to Rani, covering her capsule in a lively carpet of bees, fanning their wings and crawling eagerly over one another. My eyes course across the scene searching for telltale signs of rejection. I can see none. The Findhorn bees are accepting Rani as their new queen. I exhale and notice that Helen is calm beside me. She gently caresses the throng of bees off the cage to release Rani. The drones and workers toddle about their new queen, yearning to be near her and learn her scent. We watch her move purposefully and regally through the crowd.

Relief and grief flood me in equal measure. What now? Rani's accepted and settled. She's found her purpose and, in the process, I've lost mine. My immediate impulse is to run and I move backward away from the hives. Helen understands and lets me go without a word. I pivot and strike out away from the settlement toward the sea. I need to grieve and be in Now. Now is not always comfortable, but it's real and true.

When I reach the shore, I slow to a walk. I pass the King Fisher's throne and search for stones to skip on the flat sea. I wish Abram were with me. Hasta would love this, too, and if she were here, we would strip off our clothes and splash into the sea for a very chilly dip. Imagining Hasta makes me feel a little lighter and I fling a flat stone outward and get seven skips. That might be my record. The sun glides into the sea and I wait until the sky darkens before heading back. My neck hairs rise as I turn away from the sea. Moving in slow motion, I catch a glimpse of a shadowy form beside the Fisher King's throne.

It's the size of a large dog and as still as the driftwood statue, but definitely alive. Goosebumps race down my spine and back up again. What is it? A feral dog or a wolf? I move backwards toward the water's edge, not sure what I'm intending to do since I can't escape by way of the sea. I keep my eyes on the animal and my eyes tear up from staring. I finally blink and it's gone, as if vaporized.

I stand still contemplating my options for returning to the Foundation, either through the fields or by the road. I see the lights of a car and I know for tonight I want the company of civilization. I rush toward the car lights and almost trip over a piece of driftwood as I pass the throne. Once on the road, I walk hurriedly toward the Foundation. I feel spooked and excited. What did I see?

Hack peers at me and asks me to promise her that I will not act on what she's about to tell me. I agree, careful not to promise.

"I found something on satellite near the Findhorn Foundation and it might be connected with Ext-Pest. I've seen the white van parked there twice. I'll send you the image but you can't go there. I mean it! Tell Helen what we've found and see what she wants to do about it."

What if they're holding my mother there? I have to find out. I can't be this close and not find out. Hack stares at me and shakes her head.

"I knew I shouldn't have told you before I told Helen. Or maybe never told you at all. You cannot investigate on your own. It's too dangerous. They may be idiots, but they are dangerous idiots."

"Did you get any info from the van or about the two men?"

"Don't worry. They can't get into the Foundation. But be sure that you don't go off the grounds, in case they're watching you. Stay on the Foundation's land."

"Okay. And I'll tell Helen." I will tell her. After I check it out. I'm looking at the satellite image and already calculating how far it is from the Foundation. It's near Cluny Hill, through the woods, so I could just take a peek on my run. What if my mother is trapped in there? And I could get her out. I have to try.

I lie in the grass on my stomach and watch the lab, trying to be patient and to remember that you can't rush reconnaissance. After two hours, there's still no one around and no white van in sight. Even though I'm at rest, my heart is beating too fast. Part of my racing heart is guilt over ignoring Hack's warning and, the other part, is my drive to know what's going on inside the gray building. I move to all fours to crawl closer and suddenly every hair on my body is alert. I am being watched. Slowly, I swivel my head to look just as a low rumbling growl reaches my ears.

It's the same animal I saw at the shore, but it's not a dog or a wolf. It's a fox, a huge fox. And a vixen. I know foxes from home and I have never seen one so big, especially a female. I freeze in my tracks and wonder if I should stay on all fours or stand up. I don't want to threaten her. Crawling backwards, I edge away from the lab, and the fox watches me and snorts. Even though the sound is much friendlier than her growl, I keep moving backwards until I can't go any further without bumping into the trees. When I look for her again, she's gone. Unnerved and dissatisfied, I head back to the settlement. I can't help feeling that the vixen was not threatening me, but warning me to stay away from the lab.

I decide to take the long route to meet the twins for daily lessons. Today I want to linger in the gardens and relish feeling at home. The insects and plants are thriving in the same atmosphere of love and support as in the Compound. They sense that they are cherished and protected. The very definition of home is a place where you can feel safe and be yourself. Plants, insects and all of life experience the same distress when being shunned or mistreated. My mother knew this and created her own Findhorn. I can't wait to tell the others at home that we have a sister community across the globe.

The twins are already there, waiting for me by the hives. I look from one sister to the other. "Alright now. Tell me, what is going on with your bees?"

"Well, you probably know the Russian bees are known for their resistance to the trachea mites."

I nod at Svetlana. I know all about the bees of Vladivostok that are famous for their strong immune systems.

Dania takes over from her sister, her words rushing out. "Not anymore. The weather changes have weakened their immune systems and the mites have multiplied. We are losing hundreds of bees a day. We have tried so many things and are hoping that you can help us figure out what could help them recover."

I try to picture our thriving bee populations at the Compound in the midst of a devastating die-off. "I'll do whatever I can. When did it start?"

Dania's forehead creases and Svetlana leans forward and places a hand on her sister's knee. "I'll tell her. After our last winter. It was warmer than ever. The bees aren't adjusting to the rising temperatures. And they haven't been able to produce a queen."

"We might try taking a queen from Findhorn, where the climate is milder than in Vladivostok, to see if that helps them adjust. The bees we have at the Compound are hybrids of three different species. Actually four, since the African bee came to the U.S. The African bee genome helped our bees adapt and thrive, so maybe we can do the same for yours."

Dania agrees and a smile blooms on her face. "You know so much about bees. How old were you when you started tending them?"

"I was twelve when I was put in charge of two of the hives. Q was a brand-new queen and I was a brand-new warden. Our connection was immediate and the telepathy between us grew from there. We made up games to play. My mother had taught me about a bee's ability to scope out new sources of nectar and I wanted to try it out on Q's hive. Soon we had a favorite game, hide and seek the nectar. I'd take a solution of sugar water and go somewhere on the Compound, then wait. Within minutes, Q would arrive with a swarm of worker bees and they'd drink their fill and carry it back to the hive." Memories of Q flood my mind and I have to push them down to keep a firm grasp on Alexa. Sharing Gaia's world with the twins while keeping Alexa in charge is a new experience that Quince did not foresee. The twins seem oblivious to my inner struggle and Svetlana interrupts my thoughts.

"How do you think the telepathy works between us and other species?"

"Telepathy is based on electrical pulses. All you need is a transmitter and a receiver with current in between. Humans and bees both generate electrical current, the kind of current that doesn't need wires or fiber optics for transmission. And the waves can travel great distances which means that we don't need to be near each other to connect. Einstein called this phenomenon 'spooky action at a distance' because he couldn't explain nonlocality with the quantum physics of the time. Now we know that space is not what we once thought it was: a deterrent to instantaneous communication between particles. We now know that particles move faster than the speed of light. At the time of Einstein, it didn't make sense that particles light years apart in other solar systems could communicate with each other instantaneously. Now we know they can.

"So why don't we practice that skill here within the earth's sphere? The government would try to convince us that we don't have the power to communicate over distances or with other species. But we do. We have to go beyond the government's laws and believe in the more powerful and enduring laws of Nature. Electrical pulses attract connection. We can connect with all beings using electrical pulses."

"I want that connection, too." Dania's desire emanates from her whole being.

"I'll teach you both. I truly respect bees, maybe more than I respect humans. There's a big difference between the bees and us. They think about whether the instruction given by the hive collective makes sense before they act on it. We follow the crowd whether it makes sense for the good of all. Hack discovered a curious experiment online that showed exactly this. Bees are master navigators with excellent internal mapping abilities and can communicate the locations of nectar sources to each other. They do a waggle dance by rotating in different directions to indicate distance and location to new sources of nectar.

"In the experiment, a nectar source was moved each day to a random location and the bee scouts always found it. The scouts returned to the hive with the location, and worker bees took off to gather nectar. This happened without fail for several weeks until the experimenter put a nectar source in a boat in the middle of a lake. When the bee scouts reported the location back to the hive, the workers didn't follow up on it. They collectively decided it wasn't a practical location and they ignored the scouts' report.

"We are more impulsive and irrational than bees. We follow the human hive mentality wherever it goes, without thinking. Bees stop and consider before they follow the hive directive. I wish we did that more of the time."

Rani appears out of nowhere and hovers over our heads. Rare tears rise up in the twins' eyes. The electrical charge coming off the three of us grows stronger, reminding me of the energy of my team at training. Focused, intent and unified. Hack was right. She said that I would know whether the twins carry the intensity of commitment and the depth of heart needed for the Cause. They do.

CHAPTER 17

I AM UNEASY AND RESTLESS. I want it to be enough that I delivered Rani and can teach the twins what I know. But I miss the Compound and my team and I miss being Gaia. I need reassurance that I had a life as Gaia and can get back to it. I unzip the inside pocket of my backpack and find my new identity pack. Hack made it for me, complete with a new passport and new finger cots. I stare at the sealed opaque pouch with the words "ERAD UOY T'NOD" written across the top. She made me promise not to look inside unless I'm forced to abandon Alexa and have to create a new identity. Quince agreed that it could confuse my memory overlay to introduce another identity into my crowded headspace before I left the Compound. When it's time for a new me, I'll have to cement the new memory overlay on my own by following her techniques. She has faith that I can do it and I'm counting on her belief in me.

I like to hold the packet to remind myself that I have a way out if things get really bad. It calms me down at the same time that it tortures me because I can't look inside. I don't like not knowing what's in it and I don't like waiting to know. I hold the packet up to my forehead and breathe, but I still feel jittery. I press the packet with my thumb and forefinger to explore the thickness of the contents. It feels thicker than a passport and a thin sheet of finger cots. Closing my eyes so I can't see Hack's warning, I break the seal, half expecting an alarm to sound. After a long pause, I move an inquiring finger into the pouch.

I was right. It isn't just one passport, it's two. And two finger print packets. Was Hack so worried about this trip that she prepared two new identities for me? My curiosity overwhelms my guilt and I extract one of the passports. I tell myself I'll just glance at my photo, without looking at the name. At least, that's my plan so far. I peek inside the blue binding and my mother's face stares back at me.

Why am I carrying a passport for my mother? It can only mean that someone believes she's still alive. My hand is numb when I guide the passport back into the holder. I can't talk to anyone about this because I'm not supposed to know. Someone thinks my mother is alive.

"Abram. Abram, wake up."

"What is it?"

"It's alright, you're alright. You were talking in your sleep again. Or rather shouting."

"Oh, sorry!"

"It's okay. Come here."

Chas gathers me up like I'm breakable and draws me onto his chest. His bulk is warm and damp and he smells of musk. I breathe him in and am more aware than ever that I am completely turned on. I lift up and gripping him by the biceps, press him into the bed.

"What was I yelling?"

"You said one word: 'Gaia.' Over and over."

"Gaia? Is she a goddess?"

"I don't know."

Without warning, Chas flips me over and the bulk of his body covers me.

"Now that we're awake . . ."

"Yes!" I love this man, so much. More and more.

Gaia. I do a search for her to find that she's the goddess of Earth and mother of the Titans, the Giants and the sea. She's known as the Mother of All. I shouted out to the Mother of All in my sleep? That's blazar! What do I need from her? Or maybe I can do something for her. Maybe I can compose some music for her.

Lifting up my guitar, I strum idly and end up playing the song I taught Alexa. Inspired by her courage and strength, I venture out, letting G-C-D lead the way. New chords push their way up and I stop to write down a phrase. And another and another. The rich and stormy resonance shifts to a timbre that is light as air. It reminds me of sex this morning with Chas, and thoughts of him bring a cello accompaniment into my head, perfect for him to play. I quickly scribble it down before I lose it. Where is this coming from? I don't care. I love it.

I replay what I've written, adding the cello in my mind. Something's missing. It needs something more. Then I hear it. Alexa and the ukulele. Memory of her halting chords thread through the melody. Just a line or two. The ukulele and the cello are an unlikely pair, but they work. Another thought erupts. What about the track of ambient sounds from Alexa? Start and end the piece with crickets and cicadas and I have a song for her and Gaia. I'd like to name the piece for Alexa, but I can't risk bringing attention to her. I'll call it "Gaia's Song." And tell Alexa that she inspired me.

After seeing the photo of my mother, I can't sleep so I'm going for a night run. It's pitch-dark with no moon and I think it's best to take my headlamp and my compass. I want to run without thinking, and this way I can find my way back. I cradle the compass in my hand and tighten my fist around it. It is very special to me.

A friend of my mother's heard about a bee enthusiast who knew of my father's scientific studies and had bought some of his belongings. Our friend made the contact and when she explained to him who my mother was, the collector gifted the compass to her. My mother gave it to me when I was five when it had become obvious to her that I needed help finding my way. I was always getting lost. The collector kept in touch with us and, at my next birthday, he sent my father's handwritten paper on hive cooperation, and the following year, my father's field notebook, full of illustrations of plants and insects.

The man is named William, but I call him Uncle Billy. I don't think I'll ever get a chance to meet him and tell him how much my father's treasures mean to me. If my father were alive, he'd be in the Cause. He was for the Cause before it was the Cause. I cup the compass in my hand, warming the metal in my palm. I wonder if the compass, so worn by his touch, confirms my guess that, like me, he was directionally challenged.

I strike out over the dunes with the sea at my back. The terrain undulates in waves. An imprint of the sea is in the roll of the hills, as if the land remembers being underwater. The play of the wind pushes me back and forth, as if it's having fun trying to knock me over. I have to concentrate and ground each footfall to stay upright. As I come over a small rise, I see a shape and a flash of fur. For an instant, I think of the white-tailed deer at home, but then I remember the fox at the Fisher's throne and then again at the lab.

She is alerted and I slow to a walk, trying not to frighten her away. When my headlamp catches her in the beam of light, I can make out the white markings around the eyes. I blink and she disappears, melting into the hills. I swivel my head back and forth, casting the beam of light over the empty landscape. Excitement and fear combine to give me a shot of adrenaline that drives me for the rest of my run. I want to meet her again.

Abram and Chas sit in silence after the recorded symphony of guitar, ukulele, cello, cicadas and crickets dies away.

"It's beautiful, Abram. We have to take it to Alexa. Let's go this weekend. It's our only free weekend for months."

"Are you sure? After what happened on my last trip there?"

"Especially after what happened. We need to be sure she's okay. Don't you think this is why Findhorn traded your car for one of theirs? So that you could come back and see Alexa without worrying about being followed."

"I don't know. I don't like thinking of you getting involved."

"I am involved. I think we should go. It's so rare we both have a free weekend."

"Chas?"

"Yeah?"

"Have I told you I love you lately?"

"Uhmmm. Yesterday, I think."

"Well, I do. Shall we tell her we're coming?"

"Let's just go. You know she'll be there. She can't go anywhere right now."

"Okay! We'll surprise her. Hack can make the arrangements for us so the Foundation is expecting us."

I now have two Russian sisters. They are learning so fast it's hard for me to find new practices for them. I know about being the oldest sister on the Compound and teaching the younger ones, but with the Russians I have to be their Quince. I try to think like her and teach them what I've learned. After all, that's really all a teacher does: learns something new, then turns around and shares it.

Dania and Svetlana, eager and hard-working, are so like Hasta and me. They even argue like we do. They both ask hard questions, especially Dania. I've missed having sisters who work hard with me and then can share a silly joke. Because of the twins, I have a purpose: to help them help their bees. I am giving them everything I know and I am learning more by being with them. I'm helping to create more bee and butterfly whisperers. When I arrive, Svetlana and Dania are already at the hives, sitting in a shady spot with notebooks on their laps and their pens poised. Their readiness inspires me to jump right in.

"The very first rule of Mind Command is: be suspicious of your thoughts. Not emotions, because they are genuine feedback. I always take note of them. Like the weather, emotions are natural and innocent of guile. It's what we do with them that's important. That's the tricky part. My emotions are my individual weather system, colored and influenced by my history.

"Why am I talking about emotions in Mind Command? I'm not really off topic because you can't be successful at Mind Command if you don't know your own hot buttons. You need to familiarize yourself with your weather system to work with it. For example, is it my right to storm on someone else? If someone betrays a promise or invades a boundary, I need to say something. But otherwise, it's my weather and I'm responsible for the fallout.

"Ask yourself questions. If you feel shame, did you earn it? Or was it put on you by someone else? If so, how can you release it? If it's guilt you feel, did you stray off your path of integrity? If not, it may be anger in disguise and then you look for a responsible way to vent it. Your weather system, your responsibility.

"Now that I'm in the world I see that most people aren't taking care of their own weather systems. I can hardly believe the amount of emotional projections flying around. How do you stop from being contaminated by all that emotional debris?"

I can see by the way the twins look at each other that the answer is simple. They don't know how to stop it. I can see we need to work on filters next.

"Back to Mind Command. So, when my mind starts down a thought track, I ask myself these questions. Is it a well-worn and familiar track? Or is it new and barely etched out? What is at the end of it? A mountain? A clearing? A roadblock? A bridge? A drop-off? When I have all the information available to me about the thought, I decide if it's beneficial for my health and well-being. Is it bringing me information I need? If so, I continue with it. If not, I see what other thought tracks are available. If I have trouble changing the thought, I use the image of a tape measure. I press the return button and bring my mind back to square one. That way I release the old thought and can choose again. There are usually several thoughts that call to me immediately but I have to be careful. One of them may be just like the one I've rejected. I stopped the original thought for a good reason: to make a better choice.

"Then I ask my emotions for input. What am I feeling? Am I anxious, scared, tired or excited? Do I need peace, action or cooperation? Do I need company or alone time? Am I running from a feeling or moving toward a new experience? When running from something, I usually have picked a thought path that's full of potholes and ruts. Moving toward something new, I am choosing a path that leads me toward growth. Emotions are genuine and they help guide me but true Mind Command is about taking charge of my thoughts. I am the driver and I have to rule them or they will rule me.

"Thoughts of Now are my best ones. Now is whatever is before me. Even if I face death, Now is alive. Now has no agenda, except to be present with what is. I want to be in Now as much as possible. Beware of thought roads that have signs that say they are Now, but they are hoaxes because goals are attached. Now is not about a goal.

"At first, I was scared I would stop trying anything difficult or new if I didn't have a future goal in mind, but the opposite happened. With Now, I have more energy for moving forward on the thought tracks that are best for me. I'm more myself and less a blind follower. I get more done that is valuable and vital. I follow Now to Next.

"I remember my mother telling me that we are constantly coming to crossroads in life, but we barrel through the stop signs, missing the other roads around us. Stop and choose consciously which road to take. After you choose, see what happens and learn from it. Then choose again. Many times a day, an hour, a minute. Choose and re-choose your thoughts.

"I kept telling my mom when I was little that my thoughts just went wherever they wanted to and I didn't have a choice. She was patient with me, even when I resisted learning how to take control of them. Now I understand. A thought is a road and there are many to choose from. It's funny she taught me about roads when I never got to ride on them. Sure, there are a few dirt roads where I live, but they are very few and very short. The world of thoughts is so complex, like a country with more roads than can be counted or mapped. Thoughts can be overwhelming if not paired with your breath. I breathe and find Now. Now always brings me a better road to follow."

"How does your Mind Command bring communication with other species?" Svetlana's pen is poised over her notebook, ready to write down every word that I say.

"How can you know another species if you don't know yourself? I believe that if you spend enough time studying your inner landscape, you gain a superpower: the ability to know other beings in their unique landscapes. All beings crave being known, even antisocial cockroaches. When you offer a species connection, you are invited in and can navigate together toward a higher purpose. Be careful that you don't let the ego design the higher purpose. The ego has no idea what's best for you or anyone else."

CHAPTER 18

I HAVE KITCHEN DUTY FOR the first time tonight. The kitchen reminds me of home, but with louder music and more joking around. The familiar and communal air soothes me and I'm relieved to be in a collective hive of like-minded souls. I choose dishwashing for my station so I can stay in one place and out of the way of other helpers buzzing about, putting dishes away and cleaning counters. The mindless repetition of washing the dishes soothes me and I like watching them pile up beside me, shiny and wet. After all the dishes are clean, it's time for the cookware. The pans and pots are almost as big as I am, but I'm getting the hang of it. The spray of the nozzle tickling my skin reminds me of the waterfall at home and a stab of homesickness quickly turns into fear of the future. Will Hasta and I swim under the waterfall again? The teacher becomes the student when I have to practice what I preach about Mind Command. Breathe and find Now.

The last pan is the largest one and I wrestle it into the oversized sink. My jaw tightens to help my arms with the slippery pan. I remember that I don't need a clenched jaw to lift the pan. I soften my tongue and slip into a softer mode, and the pan relaxes in my grasp. Thanking the pan for holding the mounds of spinach lasagna, I rinse off the last of the suds. A helper takes it from me and I clean out the screens at the bottom of the deep sinks. My apron is soaked so I hang it on a hook to dry and search for Gabriel, the kitchen chief, to see if I can go. He nods to me and I slip out the door into the evening air.

I really want to skip the community meeting tonight. I had planned to go to my room and fall into bed until Helen found me at dinner and asked me to sit with her in the hall. I can't refuse her, so I'm going. I'm so exhausted, not only from kitchen duty, but from everything. Do I tell Helen about the fox? I feel guilty about not telling her about spying on the lab. Do I keep these secrets? I don't know what's right.

I breathe in the night air to give me energy for the meeting and I pull in as many antennae as I can. When I'm this tired I can't contain them as well and, when a few scattered zaps of electricity greet me at the door, my hair rustles and shifts. I'm glad that I have it in braids to save me the embarrassment of a full-blown liftoff. The air in the hall is supercharged and I send long roots down through the floorboards to anchor myself. The Great Hall fills up and thrums with streams of conversation. I think the whole community must be here. Helen's pleasure at having me beside her makes being in such a big crowd a little easier. She keeps one hand on my arm as if she's afraid I'll escape. Her touch is motherly and comforting and soothes my jumpy nerves.

The noise ebbs away as soon as Carla starts the meditation and makes the call for the Unseen Ones. I love this part of being at the Findhorn Foundation and feel as if I have been doing it my whole life without naming it. First, we breathe, calming the mind and drawing it away from everyday worries. Then comes the request: an invitation to all and any Unseen Ones that can help us preserve the balance and health of the planet and encourage a new human consciousness to ensure a positive and sustainable future. Then there is silence for our own personal communion with the Unseen Ones. Mine is always the same. "Nature, please give us more time. We are slow and stubborn, but there is good in our hearts. Please don't give up on us."

Carla's call is answered. The air is quickly crowded with Unseen Ones and the hall keeps expanding to accommodate all of our guests. The ends of the hall stretch and elongate until we are encapsulated in a multitude of loving presences. The silence pulses in my ears, creating a comforting throb. I tremble with the mounting vibrations. I am a tuning fork and my bones are the prongs.

The call for the Unseen Ones always affects me, but tonight I am more sensitive than usual to their arrival. An etheric partition surrounds me, cutting me off from those around me. I feel all alone in the crowded hall when one entity selects me and wraps an energy force around me. I lean into the comforting male presence and as tears well up in my eyes, he whisper his name to me, "I am the Comforter." I hear crickets and cicadas and wonder if he is transporting me home for an out-of-body visit to treat my homesickness. I'm immersed in a summer evening with Hasta when Helen lays a cool hand on my arm. My eyes startle open.

My brother is in the center of the hall with two men, and they are playing the most beautiful song I've ever heard. I am laughing and crying. The insect recording that I shared with Abram fills the hall and is joined by the musicians, one by one. First, Abram on his guitar, followed by Gabriel, the kitchen chief, on the ukulele, and finally a cello player completes the trio. The cellist, a bear of a man, has to be Chas.

Helen takes my hand and squeezes it. Now overpowers me and leaves me speechless. I wouldn't want to be anywhere else. The melody weaves itself around the hall, sending communal shivers through the crowd. My heart, already full before the music began, overflows into tears once more. When the last of the cicadas' sonorous song dies away, Abram speaks into the microphone.

"We call this piece 'Gaia's Song.' It's for our Mother, the Earth, and for all she gives us without asking for anything in return, except our respect. I am Alexa's brother and am glad to be able to share this song with all of you."

"Gaia's Song"?! Holy Blazar Quark! My brother is not only a class-A musician, but also a sentient. Rani is not with me, but a phantom bee paces on my scalp and shivers race up and down my spine. The conversational buzz around me rivals the drone of the bees. Helen peels away from me and I'm quickly overtaken by people asking me about Abram. Still in shock, I keep trying to make my way to the center of the hall to reach him. I can barely see him beyond all of the people streaming down from their seats. I keep nodding and smiling and saying yes to all of their questions. Abram finally spots me, over the heads that are peppering both of us with curious questions.

Chas gets to me before I make it to Abram. He comes from my left and facing me, he pulls me toward him and I'm suddenly being hugged by a bear that plays the cello like an angel. He squeezes me tightly and I think of the Comforter whose protective energy held me minutes before. I hope this is a trend that will go on, protective and loving holding. The next moment, Abram has me in his arms.

I slip between Abram and Chas and we walk the short way from the hall to the fire pit behind the pottery studio. Dania and Svetlana are already seated around the lit fire. It needs more fuel, so I grab a small log and place it on the embers. "Abram, you remember Dania and Svetlana."

Chas catches the sheepish look shared by the two women and he perks up.

"Are you the two with car trouble?"

"Uh-huh."

"We are really sorry . . ."

Abram leans toward the girls. "Don't worry about Chas. He's just curious, not judgmental. So, are you learning all about bees from my sister?"

"So much! She is so good with them."

"I thought I knew bees until I met her."

I have to jump into this conversation. "These two are the amazing ones! I wish I could learn as quickly as they do. Rani has bonded with both of them and we are already working on a young queen for them to take back to Russia."

"How strict are the insect laws in Russia?" Curious, Chas leans in to hear the answer to his question.

"It's not quite as bad as the U.S. but we are headed in that direction. It's only because our government is not as organized and we are dealing with so much poverty and rebellions. But we are trying to plan for the future and be as established as we can before it gets worse."

"We are so grateful that Alexa is willing to help us."

I feel embarrassed by the praise and start to deflect it with some humor when I stop my thought track. Instead, I look at each person sitting with me around the fire. First Abram, with his easy grin, then Chas, who has one hand on Abram's knee. Next Svetlana, staring into the flames, her chin in her palms, and Dania, always ready to meet my gaze. Now is where I am. For a moment, I forget about the Compound. I am Now. Abram hands me the ukulele and picks up his guitar.

"Do you want to try our road trip song?"

"Yep. I'll try."

"So, let me hear a little about each of you. Dania, you first. Just try giving me a nutshell description of who you are." We are meeting for class in the Original Garden and each of us is cradling a newly-fallen apple.

"From the time I was little, I wanted to live in the trees and I dreamt of being in a jungle tribe. I wanted to bathe in streams and eat off the land. I am always outside and finding ways to be in nature more and more. I have trouble with walls, houses, schedules and organizing." Dania finishes off by taking an ample bite of her apple.

"Good. And you, Svetlana?"

"I wanted to learn all I could, all the facts in all the books. We had a set of encyclopedias in our home and I read all the volumes from A to R. I want to know the why and how of everything. My logic is strong and I catalogue all that I read. My intuition is weaker and more foreign to me."

"You both did something self-aware and admirable by stating your weaknesses along with your strengths. It's good that you always keep sight of your weak areas because if you don't know them, how can you strengthen them? My weakness is waiting and not knowing so I am working on gaining patience.

"Know your shadow. Your shadow is the part of you that you shy away from. You can find it by looking at the judgments you have about others. We can find our shadow in the things that bother us the most. It's all there in your projections on other people. If you deny a part of yourself, you will ultimately project it onto others. That's a good definition of war: the projection of a country's shadow onto another country or people with the intent to destroy that shadow. But you can't annihilate your shadow, you have to befriend it. It's your humanity. Reject it and you lose part of your humanity. The loss of humanity is what makes war and the destruction of Nature possible.

"The bee connection was always there for me. I have always communicated with insects, and other animals, anything sentient, trees and plants and even inanimate objects. I don't know how I do it. I can teach you what I was taught. The rest is up to you." I pause, wanting to hone in on the most salient part of my connection to other beings. Intense scenes pop into my mind: Q going over the gate, news of my mother missing—and the accompanying feelings of grief and terror. I suddenly know what I need to tell the twins.

"I felt it from the very beginning. Mind Command is part of it, but I've been trying to figure out how to teach you the part that was always there. I know that you have to know your thought tracks and have control over them. I know you have to breathe consciously, clear out fears and take responsibility for your emotions. I can teach you those things. But the next step? I'm not sure, but I think it's empathy. You have to be willing to move into another realm and leave your familiar world behind. Being a bee is very different than being a human being. You bring back something from each new encounter, something that makes you bigger. Not greater, just bigger. More expansive.

"The last piece is the hardest. It's about the heart. The heart is breakable and you have to accept that. You can't be afraid to have your heart broken into pieces, over and over again. You have to trust that it was made to rupture and repair. You have to risk. I don't know how to prepare you for that. Life has already tested you with your own personal trials, traumas and losses. I'm guessing that you two have had plenty of those lessons."

The sisters nod in unison.

"Number 1: Mind Command is your boundary. Number 2: Empathy is your connector. Number 3: Risking your heart is your vulnerability. Then back to step 1 and repeat, over and over again. Let's go to the bees now and start your first lesson. As we get closer to the hive, transmit this thought: 'I'm here to know you.'"

We walk in silence and circle the hive. Moving slowly and deliberately, I gently lift the wooden frame and allow the bees to explore the spaces in between my fingers. The familiarity of the tickle thrills me. "If a bee evades your touch, let it move away. Watch me and imagine yourself doing what I'm doing. Keep your hands soft. See yourself relaxed and happy to be sharing the touch of bees. Your intent is everything. You come to them open and interested. Feel the delicate feet and the fanning wings. Your work tonight is to replay this moment over and over again in your head. You're not threatened or threatening. Any questions?"

The twins are moved to stillness, intently watching the bees. I rest the back of my hands on the frame and the colony shifts toward the wooden edge. One stays behind after the others have moved on. I lift up my hand to gaze into the eyes of a curious young drone. I lower my hand to bring the bee close to my heart. My heart beats steadily and strong in Now. After a few moments, the drone lifts off and returns home. "Nature's creatures know and understand Now better than we ever will."

Dania reaches out, as if in a trance, to stroke my hands, wanting to feel their softness. She's the tactile one. Svetlana is more mental and, with eyes closed, is moving her hands in imitation of mine, sifting through a pool of imaginary bees.

Dania's touch is so receptive that I know the bees will receive her. I direct her hands toward the hive and look to see if she's ready to try. She nods, and the confidence in her nod lets me know she's ready. I lift a frame and guide her hands toward it. Cupping her hands in mine, we move together into the cluster of bees until the thrill of it overtakes her and I slowly move away. She relates to them with the calm of a seasoned apiarist. Svetlana watches with wide eyes and the unenvying love of a sister. Dania grins at me and I grin back. I'm learning so much about them as I watch them with the bees. Respect and intent. Intent and respect.

CHAPTER 19

"ALEXA, LET'S TAKE CHAS TO meet Rani."

"Yes, I'd love to meet a queen bee."

"I'll take you both there now. But remember that she's just gotten settled in her new hive and may be distracted, so we'll have to play it by ear. She takes her role as queen very seriously."

I send Rani a telepathic heads-up that Abram, Chas and I are on our way. I can sense her moving through the throng of bees to the top surface of the frame, and when we arrive, she is emerging from the hive. I gesture for Chas to stand beside me. Even before she completely appears, I hear her piping, a beautiful sustained note of authority and contentment.

"Why, that's a perfect G#!" Chas leans toward Rani and she lifts off the screen to land on his head. She taps two times and Chas closes his eyes, coming down on his knees. She pipes again, her perfect G# and he grins, anchored to the spot.

"You're right, Abram. This is blazar!"

I'm hanging up my apron in the kitchen after lunch when Abram appears.

"Alexa, have you seen Chas?"

"No, where did you see him last?"

"He went back to our room to get something while I was helping in the garden. But he hasn't come back yet."

"Come with me to check on the hives and then we'll look for him."

As we near the hives, resonant, rich chords rumble toward us, long and held. The automatic impulse not to disturb something sacred freezes us in our tracks. We watch Chas from a distance and let the vibrations waft over us. He is settled on a tree stump near the hives, embracing his cello with one arm while the other dances with the bow. The bees are in a heightened state of joy, lifting off and alighting once more on top of the hives, reminding me of popcorn over a fire.

As we listen, wisps of my hair stir and rise. Rani lifts off to settle on the bow. Her antennae vibrate and sway with the sweep of his arm. I suddenly have an idea. I move close enough to reach out and touch the bridge of his cello and the volume swells. Chas's eyes widen in surprise and he glances down at his instrument. I withdraw my hand and it returns to acoustic. I connect again and the sound swells, filling our ears with the hum and whine of a thousand bees singing through the strings.

Mesmerized, Chas plows ahead, quickening the tempo, and I place two hands on the body of his cello. The whole hive swarms, ecstatic to find a giant sound source like its own. Chas plucks and strikes the strings, causing the bees to waggle and dance. The cello's voice magnifies and Chas draws out a G# until the suspense is nearly unbearable before finally drawing his bow away. Mimicking the cello, Rani sounds the G# and rises off the bow, swooping and swaying in midair like a conductor leading her orchestra. The swarm of bees join her in song and I bring my hands together in the gesture of honor. Something much larger than music, electricity and bees is at hand. It is the two Shes, Nature and Earth, combining their magnificence in a concert for us. Music is Now. It doesn't know anywhere else to be. And when we join the music, we join Now.

Chas reaches out to touch my hands and I pull them away quickly before he reaches me. I don't want to shock him any more than I already have. He doesn't say a word, just looks at Abram and back at me. I don't think he knows that Rani is sitting on top of his head.

"Tell Chas about it, Alexa."

"My mother noticed something odd about me when I was very little. I would run up to share some exciting news and when I was near anything electrical, it would spark or blow a fuse. And not only was electricity sensitive to me, I was sensitive to it. I was terrified of lightning. If I heard thunder, my heart would race and I'd run to hide under the bed. Once, I fainted when a bolt of lightning hit very close to the house. We never knew if I fainted from fear or the electrical blast.

"She did everything she could think of to protect me. She taught me how to ground myself and how to conserve the extra energy that would build up in me. I could store it for later or release it if it made me jumpy.

I'm better now but I still get nervous when I hear thunder. Water soothed me and my mother knew to put my wrists under cool water or send me to the pond to discharge the current. I guess I was a little like an electric eel, hot-wired and still at home in the water. Did you know that electric eels can electrocute themselves? They know how to avoid it but it can happen accidentally if their own tail makes contact with them. Isn't it weird that your gift can end up killing you?"

"And you used your superpower to electrify my cello? That's so gen. You know, it makes sense to me, that a superpower has to be watched so it doesn't take over and turn on you. It's a big responsibility."

"I'm not sure it's a superpower. Have you ever known, without looking, that someone is staring at you from behind? You don't see them, you sense them. That's electroreception. You are picking up the charge of their stare. Human beings still have that sense. It's just that most of you don't use it. The enormous amount of electrical charge coming from the world has numbed you to the more subtle waves that surround us. When we notice those waves, we get signals, like knowing when a deer is nearby and ready to leap across our path or when a plant needs water. If we ignore these signals, we ignore our own nature. And everything around us will suffer. Our nature is to tend, share, receive and care. We are electrically wired to do that. Life is complicated, unpredictable and chaotic. But if you pay attention, it all makes sense. If you don't, you miss so much."

Chas leans his cello against a tree and turns toward me. "You think we all have it?"

"Yes, I don't think I'm special. I think we can all remember electroreception. Ancient humans needed it to stay safe from predators and predict bad weather. When we find your switch, we can turn it on for you. Maybe fear of power is in the way or a belief system that thinks it's impossible. Belief and ability are key."

"What is blocking me?" Abram turns toward me and I can tell he really wants to know. A courageous and vulnerable aura surrounds him.

"For you, I think you guard and control your musical talent closely and will do anything you can to keep it safe, because it's so important to you. Do you think that having this ability could harm your music?"

"Maybe. I'm not sure what would happen if I tapped into it. Could I electrocute myself like the electric eel?"

"I don't think that would happen. But you have to risk not knowing what could happen. I believe tapping into it would only make you more sensitive and give you more access to the music of the spheres. You know, as a musician, that music doesn't come from the Earth, right? Most of it comes from beyond this plane, so your talent could grow exponentially. You'd have to risk it. Like you did when you had the Gaia dream. That dream and your song for Gaia came from somewhere beyond what we can see or touch."

"I want to know more. I want to know because I love you and want to know you better."

My heart blooms whenever Abram talks about loving me. And then I think about losing him and I remind myself to watch my own thought tracks. I have to risk loving him, even though I've lost people I love and the pain of those losses is still sharp. I have to keep risking or I'll lose the most important thing I have, my humanity. Without that, I lose my connection with the bees. "Abram, we need to take it slowly because right now your electrical system is busy keeping your heart pumping and sending the right signals to your brain. We don't want to overload your system, so for today, let's start with your antennae."

"My antennae?"

"Actually, just think of your hair. Have you ever rubbed a balloon on your head and your hair stood up? And when you get a chill or see something amazing the hair on your arms rises up?"

"Oh, yeah."

"Well, it's the same principle. There are electrical charges around us all the time. Electromagnetism is one of the four forces of nature, like gravity. Sea turtles and dolphins use it to navigate and eels and anteaters use it to find food. We may have had, in the past, the same electroreceptors in our noses that anteaters have in their snouts. Like theirs, our trigeminal nerve runs through our senses—our eyes, nose and mouth.

"Our brains fire with electricity and we are wired to detect supercharged ions coming our way. When someone is angry or aggressive, the ionic impulse increases and we can make choices before the aggression follows the charge. It's all about charges, negative and positive, and the subtle signals that are emanating from everything. When you become more sensitized, you can pick up signals from everything around you whether animate and inanimate.

"Close your eyes and feel the connection between your hair and your brain. Focus on the current naturally running through your skull and through your brain tissues. Remember the feeling of the hair rising on the back of your neck. Simulate it now by thinking of something surprising or exciting, like Chas and his electric cello. Feel it and you activate your antennae. You can do this even if you're bald, because it's not really the hair doing it. Well, for bees, it is the actual hairs being charged by motion. But for us, it's invisible antennae that are forever reaching for something beyond what we can see, touch or even know. Just like music is able to communicate something that words can't."

"I think I can feel it."

"Hold that feeling. Call it up and ask your antennae to reach as far as they can. And remember, you are safe and your music is safe."

Abram's hair floats up half an inch. He shivers and it lifts a bit more and when he opens his eyes, his gaze is clear and innocent, like a newborn. "That feels great!"

"That's enough for now. Just a little every day so your system gets used to it. You've heard of kundalini nerve damage? It's a real thing. Too much, too fast and you send your system into shock and overload. You don't want to be a rogue electric eel!"

My day is full with working in the Original Garden. I can't believe how starved I am to have dirt between my fingers, to touch delicate green shoots and commune with Scottish dragonflies that are every bit like ours at home. I miss home today, but everyone here is so kind and friendly, the ache is waning. I'm feeling that good kind of tired that leads to a solid night's sleep. Sleep makes me think of holding Hasta before I left, and those tender thoughts bring up my mother. I lean closer to the pea shoots beneath me. Tears drop on the leaves before I register any feeling of sadness. I am raining on the peas. My tears make me think of Dorothy.

When the Original Garden first began to flower, Dorothy Maclean spent a day communing with her pea plants. She learned from continual communication with them that peas longed for sympathy. She discovered that peas are very sensitive plants, vulnerable to insult and aggression. Longing for kindness, they loved to talk to her. "Humans generally seem not to know where they are going or why." That was a message Dorothy heard from a very perceptive pea plant in her garden.

I lift my face away from the pea vine and my tears stop. I lean in and they flow. The back and forth movement turns my tears off and on like a faucet. Pea plants make me cry. I'll have to tell Amey to be especially nice to the pea plants at home. A squash blossom beside the pea vine shifts ever so slightly on its stem and I caress the delicate edge of the large white petals. "You are a beauty," I tell her. She seems to grow a bit, swelling at her center. I am entranced, tingling from scalp to toes. I'm concentrating so hard on the blossom that it takes me longer than usual to sense a presence nearby. Scanning around me, my gaze falls on the fox. What is she doing here?

She tracks my approach and I wonder why I'm walking steadily toward such a large and wild creature. I pause several yards away to telegraph a friendly greeting. A turn of her ears signals her interest in me and her relaxed posture intimates her trust in me. I hold my hands palms up, fingers touching as a gesture of peace, and she rises up and comes toward me. I stay very still, my heart pulsing against my jacket. The fox sniffs my outstretched fingers, her nose moist and soft. She raises her eyes to mine, tilting her head side to side as if she's memorizing the contours of my face. Her tail swishes before she moves backwards. And before I can exhale, she's gone, melting into the rows of vegetables and flowers around us. The Findhorn gardens are famous for forty-five-pound cabbages but I never thought I would meet a forty-five-pound fox here. I recall her breath on my fingertips. A perfect mix of wild and gentle. I hope I see her again.

I just asked Dania and Svetlana if they wanted to go for a run with me after class and they said no, they couldn't. Which is okay, except that something was strange. They were hiding something from me. I feel uneasy because I want to trust them and I want them to trust me. Their collective no keeps bothering me during my run. I can't figure out if I feel rejected by them or frustrated that I can't figure them out. Which is worse? I think it's not figuring them out. I try to use the inner tape measure but I can't switch thought tracks. I change my route and run out toward the Fisher King's throne to skip some stones. That always helps me shift to a better place.

The mud flats stretch out before me. The sea plants are shiny with rain and I ask permission to pluck a leaf. The salty burst reminds me of my first day at the Foundation, still groggy from chloroform and reeling from the escape. I smile thinking of Abram beside the throne that day. I gather some flat stones into a pile by the water's edge and prepare for my first launch. As I am positioning the rock in my hand, I spy a sea creature—no, two sea creatures in the calm beyond the waves. Squinting to focus, I try to remember what animals would be in the North Sea: seals, whales and dolphins. But the creatures are swimming with front flippers rising up rhythmically and consistently. As I hone in closer on the two images, I suddenly see that it's Dania and Svetlana. So, this is what the awkwardness was about. Were they embarrassed to be going for a swim in the frigid North Sea or sorry they couldn't ask me to participate? And why not? Why wouldn't I want to join them in an arctic swim? I dip my hands into the water and shiver. Those hardy Russian girls were right to exclude me. Hasta would love me in this position. She would tease me mercilessly that I have met my match with these two.

CHAPTER 20

STOPPING BY THE OFFICE, I find a note from Helen with a hand-drawn map attached. I follow the arrow on the map to arrive at a wooden house made from a giant whisky barrel. Two goats munch grass on the sod roof and they don't even look up when I knock on the round door beneath them. I wait and knock again. A man in knitted slippers and a long scarf answers the door.

"Hi. I'm Alexa. Helen sent me to see you." I have no idea why I'm here and I'm hoping he does.

"Come on in. I'm Bertie. I have cider on the stove and I've made bannock. Would you like some?"

"Yes, thank you!" I don't know what bannock is, but the aroma is enticing. Bertie's home is as warm and welcoming as he is, with a pot-bellied stove and forest green walls. Jugs and vases crowd the shelves, pushing each other aside for a place to perch. Earthen jars line the counter space, alongside of cups and pitchers with fluted lips and pots with lids with fantastical creatures perched on top. An old clock ticks loudly and the kettle shrieks, making a drum and whistle duet. I could live here.

Bertie butters the flatbread, which I guess is the bannock, and slathers on apricot jam without asking me, as if he knows apricot is my favorite. And hands me a cider cup with the plate. The crockery is smooth and round bottomed, reliable in my hands.

"So, Helen sent you. I guess I need to tell you why you're here, because I'm guessing she didn't."

"Right." Crumbs tumble from my mouth onto my lap when I speak.

"I run the earth classes. Clay, sand, mud and mineral, anything Mother Earth gives us for free. From that we can make things we need for living and for dreaming. Utility and art. Helen must want you to stay grounded and learn about what you are standing on while you're here at the Foundation."

"I think I'm pretty grounded."

"I'm sure you are if you just made that journey. This is not about a deficit. It's about adding to your experience of planet Earth. Communicating with this spot on the planet."

"I get it. I'm in my head so much of the time that I do depend on the gardens at home to settle me."

"I think that's what Helen was thinking. Come anytime you feel you need some dirt."

He smiles at me and I relax even more. I don't have to guard here.

"The first lesson is reading pots. Close your eyes and I'll put one in your hands and you tell me what you feel."

He places a bowl in my hands and I wrap my fingers around it. It tells me it comes from somewhere else. From far away and long ago. "It's not from here and it's not one of yours. It's very old and far from home."

"Good. Yes, it's two thousand years old and from China. Try this one."

I caress the smooth exterior of the bowl he hands me. The clay is from nearby, but he didn't make it. It was a woman who sculpted it and she put love into it. I have tears in my eyes when I look up. "This was made by a woman here in Findhorn. With love."

"Right again. My wife made that before she died, actually as she was dying. It's the last pot she made."

I don't know what to say so I place the bowl gently in front of him and my hands move automatically into the gesture of peace. The silence swells until he breaks it.

"So, I'm going to show you my studio and let you explore. You can use any medium or tools you find."

We climb a winding stairway up into a high tower. Sunlight streams in from tall windows and illuminates the tables strewn with tools, materials and half-finished sculptures. There's so much to take in, I'm overwhelmed, so I move to the pieces drying on the window shelf. Rows of small faces of the sun smile at me, radiant with hope. "Can I touch one?"

"Yes."

I set my palm on the hardened clay and wait. Everything has a heartbeat, no matter how inanimate it appears. It may seem inert, dry and void of life, but it is a collection of moving particles. The clay sun ripples under my hand, sending chills up from my feet. Bertie walks toward the staircase and places a hand on the railing. "I'll be back later. Take your time and don't worry about making anything. Just explore."

After a few hours in Bertie's studio, I crave fresh air. Deciding to skip the communal dinner, I walk out into the beet fields. I have no more room for people and I need a dose of Nature. The long, variegated leaves are quiet and subdued, as if they, too, have had enough. I decide that beets are either introverted and not interested in communing or weary from a day in the sun. When I get to the end of a long row, I realize that the light is fading faster than I thought and I retrace my steps to return to the settlement.

That's when I see her, the vixen. She looks up at me, a half-eaten beet in her mouth. I walk toward her knowing I may be invading her privacy but when I stop to respect her space, she tilts her head and snorts. Instead of seeming startled or wary, her tail wags like a friendly flag. "Come here!" I hear her telepath to me.

Moving slowly, I join her, selecting a beet and dropping down beside her in the dirt. I dust off the dark red root and take a bite. Then she does an odd thing. Dropping her food, she stamps the ground with her foot and turns to me expectantly. I don't know what to do, so I stand up and stamp my foot. She shakes her head in annoyance and stamps her foot again. I watch her, fascinated and confused. I jump in place, both feet going up and down. She looks at me pityingly. What is she trying to tell me?

After several minutes, she comes to me, licks the red beet stain on my fingers and saunters off into the brush. I sit down once more and watch the twilight turn into night. When I stand to go, I stamp my feet again and again, partly to warm myself and partly to try to solve the mystery of her stamping foot. The fox is probably home by now and I follow her example by taking the path toward the lights of the commune.

"Amey told me to tell you that Q is back. She also wanted to know how Rani is doing at Findhorn."

"Oh."

For a moment, I'm mad at Hack for telling me. The news from home is good, so why am I upset? Because Q is my queen and I should be greeting her when she returns.

"Alexa?"

"Yes, Hack. Thanks for letting me know. It's a relief to know she's safe. Tell Amey that Rani is completely adjusted to her new hive and that Findhorn has gracious hosts, in the hives and the houses."

Hacks laughs and has to sign off. I sit staring at my watch marking the mounting of my jealousy, resentment and homesickness. Now seems far away, so I try to pull my thoughts back with the tape measure, but I push and push the imaginary button and nothing happens. My weather front of emotions is stalled inside me and holds my thoughts hostage.

I decide to watch my physical symptoms with a curious detachment: the rush of blood to my face, the prickles of adrenaline rising on my arms and the heavy stone in my belly. I concentrate on my belly first, placing a warm hand there. I see a child curled up in a ball shielding herself against the intensity of missing her mother. I rub my stomach gently and whisper to her. "I'm here." My next breath prods the cold stone. It shrinks a little and the flush recedes from my face allowing my skin to rest easier on my muscles and bones. The urge to hide is still with me but Now is creeping back, bit by bit.

Breathing consciously reminds me of something my mother told me. "Only you can leave yourself out of your life. Once you are grown, you are the only person who can truly abandon you. The abandonment of self is the only true heartbreak." I remember my relief when she told me that. It was the day I was upset when I was left out of an outing and sat by the gate thinking I might run away. She taught me that I am responsible for including myself in whatever is happening in Now and to stay by my side wherever I am. Clarity comes with this memory, bringing Now, and the length of tape zips back into its case. I need to visit Rani and the beehives. The bees have the ability to take away my grumpiness.

On my way to Rani, I remember that I forgot to tell Hack about my dream last night. It was very real, as if I truly visited the Compound during the night. In the dream, I go to see Hack in her tech room. I know I'm not allowed there, but I am compelled to go anyway. The room is empty and in her chair is a seashell. I pick it up, put it to my ear and hear Hack calling my name. She asks me to take the seashell to the Commander and be careful not to drop it. I do what she asks but when I arrive the Commander is fast asleep. I shake her but can't wake her to tell her that I think Hack is caught in the seashell. I wake up very upset.

I dream about the Commander and the other girls often, but never Hack. Why did I dream about her now? I tap my watch to bring her back in. Nothing happens. The screen stays dark. The skin on my scalp tingles and waves of prickles roam about my head. My stomach tightens. I signal for her again and there's no response. How can that be? I just talked to her twenty minutes ago. I try again and again. What could be wrong? I need to find Helen.

I'm with Helen and we're both staring at a blank screen. It's been hours since the last contact and we haven't slept or eaten. Helen is as scared as I am and that scares me even more. She has never lost contact with the Compound for this long. Is the Compound under siege? That thought clutches my breath and holds it captive. I look at Helen and she is using all her tools to stay calm. I follow her into the sea of calm and we breathe together. I find Now for several seconds before my mind races back to panic.

I can't get home to help. Is there nothing I can do? My breath is suddenly outside of me, beyond my reach, jagged and unrecognizable. I met this same terror in the float, the annihilation of all that I love. I have to do something. I know very well that the thought track I'm on only ends in one way—with my feeling desperate and hopeless, terrified and alone. I try the measuring tape and nothing happens. I am out of tricks and heartsick. I need help. That thought brings the Comforter from the Great Hall to my side, and his expansive vortex surrounds me and speaks, "We can help."

"How!?" My tone is sharp and panicked, but my breath is returning to me slowly, regulating with the Comforter's.

"We can go there. We can help them. Can help cloak them."

"You can?! How? Never mind that. Please go. Go Now." I lean into the Comforter in relief, but he's gone and I crumple onto my side. The room echoes with a whooshing sound like so many birds taking off at once. I look at Helen to see if she heard it, too. She is deep in meditation, with eyes closed.

I stare at the darkened screen and count my breaths. Inhale—pause. Exhale—pause. Inhale—pause. Exhale—pause. I don't know how long I breathe like this before Hack appears, her face flushed and her eyes darting.

"I think we're safe. We had a surprise drone sweep so we had to shut everything down. We waited and waited and then a very weird thing happened. We heard the drones overhead and a peculiar gust of wind, then silence. As if all the drones suddenly disappeared. Then all the insects that had been silent burst into song. It was wild!"

Hack peers at me with her concerned face. "Are you okay? You look pale."

"I'm fine, just tired. We were so worried. I asked for help and they came."

"Who is 'they'?"

"The Unseen Ones. Helpers from another realm. They are here at Findhorn, but are really everywhere, all the time. And when you reach out to them, they can do their job."

"What is their job?"

"To help us. To help planet Earth."

"Thank goodness! We need it so badly. Oh, I have to run. You sure you're okay? Do you have someone there to be with you?"

"Helen is here with me and . . . more." The Comforter moves closer and warmth envelopes me. "I'm good, Hack, and I love you."

I see Hack bow her head and push a button. The heart emoji appears on my screen. Hack is back to normal. Maybe now that I'm in the outside world, Hack and I are more connected. I now live in the world that Hack knows. Her world is my Now.

Helen reaches out her arms and I melt into her warmth. She knows from her own intense love of Findhorn how worried I was about the Compound. I shift in her embrace and whisper a question I have been holding since I first saw the vixen. "Have you ever seen a fox at the Foundation?"

"No. I don't think I've seen a fox here for a very long time. Why, have you?"

"Yes, and she always seems to know where I am."

"Are you afraid of her?"

"No, it's odd. She's friendly and I think she's looking out for me."

"It looks like you've got helpers everywhere. I'll be on the lookout for your fox. Go get some food and then rest."

I don't think Helen will ever see my fox. I think the fox knows exactly what she's doing. I wish I knew what she was doing.

CHAPTER 21

I'M AGITATED AFTER HOURS OF stress about the Compound's safety. I need a run. I'm worried that I'm losing strength and endurance. I've tried to keep up my training by myself, but it's hard without the encouragement and camaraderie of my team.

I brave the cold to explore more of Cluny Hill. A bright sun tracks me from above. After four miles the Victorian hotel comes into view, sporting spires and peaked roofs at varying levels on the horizon. It's the hotel where the three founders first landed jobs and the location of a hydrotherapy retreat for health and rejuvenation that opened in 1864. It's intriguing to imagine Charles Darwin taking healing baths there.

I pass the elderly groundskeeper. In his ragged and soiled clothes, he appears to have grown right out of the garden. I cannot picture him anywhere else, dressed any differently or doing any other job. If I were told he'd been found as a baby among the giant cabbages, I would believe it.

The door to the great hall is open and the sun streams in through bubbled glass, warming the stone floors and the dark wooden panels. I stand in a square of sunlight and listen for voices or other sounds of people. The chamber is deserted except for ghosts of the past who linger in the spacious room mingling with the massive furniture.

I leave the hall to take a turn on the hill above the house, climbing higher and higher to get a bird's-eye view of the sea, charging ahead until every leg muscle strains to pull me along. I'm back at training with the girls and they are running beside me. At last, I can't push any further and with hands on my hips, I pace around in a wide circle, letting my heart ramp down. Looking at the ground as I trace and retrace the circle, I am suddenly called to look up.

The vixen is standing by an outcrop of rocks watching me. Wherever I am, there she is. I know her well enough to go to her and she meets me halfway. Kneeling down, I risk breaking a boundary and bury my head in her collar of fur. I breathe her in and she does the same to me. I breathe in again, taking in as much of her as I can. I hadn't realized how much I missed my four-legged friends and their spirits of authenticity and purity.

The vixen draws back and I release her. She turns and heads toward the rocks, glancing back once to see if I'm following her. We move up the hill and enter a clearing. She walks to the edge of a stand of trees, stops and stamps her foot. Like before. I do the same. I jump with both feet, feeling playful. She shakes her head as if to tell me this is not a game, it's serious. I stand still in front of her and she steps forward to lick my hand, showing her patience with my ignorance. What is she trying to tell me? I wish I knew. After a few moments, she trots away, giving me one backward glance. The walk back to my room is long and filled with homesick thoughts. I miss my friends and, even though I don't know her well, I miss the fox.

I'm feeling caged and my restlessness is pushing me to risk going further afield. I need new vistas for my run and so I head toward the town of Findhorn. Once over the ridge, I face the small picturesque fishing village with uniform homes and quiet streets. Separate from the Foundation, Findhorn, the town, is strictly off-limits to me. My feet propel me toward the harbor even though my mind is remembering Helen's warning to stay on Foundation land. I justify my disobedience by reminding my conscience that I left the Ext-Pest lab after that first visit and have never returned.

For a moment I feel justified even though I know the absence of one sin does not condone the allowance of another. A fog of uneasiness settles around me, dampening my runner's high with a sense of dread. I push ahead, ignoring the growing feeling that something's wrong. My mind knows what I'm supposed to do, but my feet want freedom and release. I'm too tired of being penned in to stop myself. I want to go to the end of the beach where the roiling waters turn from an inlet into a vast ocean. Ignoring more inner warnings, I urge myself to run faster to see how quickly I can get there. Not much farther now.

The road ends in a series of low dunes covered in tall sea oats. I run through the sea grasses and brush them with my hands, relishing the tickle. Over the crest of a dune, I spy the turbulent water as it crashes onto the rocky point of land. I'm mesmerized and stop to watch the inlet merge with the sea. There is water as far as I can see. The wind rips around me, reminding me of the sound of the airplane.

My heart is still pounding from running when my feet fly out from under me from a blow from behind. "Was it the wind?" is my first thought. "Don't leave the boundary!" is my second. Someone presses my face hard into the sand and I hold my breath. I am still, playing dead, waiting for my assailant to let down his guard. I'm poised to break free when a low growl erupts above me and is followed by a jarring thud. My assailant cries out at the same instant that the fox's teeth make contact.

While the two wrestle I scramble upright, looking frantically about to gage my options. The heavier of the two men is not far behind, just leaving the road to plow up the dunes. The only way out is to swim to the opposite shore. I rush to the edge and plunge in, taking long strides through the icy shallows. A drop-off surprises me and the shock of cold water hits my chest and halts my lungs in mid-inhale. I kick hard to propel myself forward. First thought: "Hasta would hate this!" Second thought: "Go, Go, Go!" The fox saved me, and now I want to save her. I scream at the top of my lungs. "FOX! COME!"

She's beside me before I can find my next breath, her tail heavy with water and blood still on her muzzle. The opposite shore moves closer and closer. She reaches the shore before me and shakes herself off, watching me fight the current. Adrenaline pulls my legs through the waist-deep waves. I glance behind me when I'm ankle-deep. Two figures on the dune watch us, too injured or too chicken to follow.

Running back to the Foundation in wet clothes is cold and miserable. The only true source of warmth I feel comes from the rush of shame that burns my cheeks. I was innocent when the kidnapping happened, but this is different. I knew better than to ignore Helen's warning. "The Foundation grounds and Cluny Hill are safe. Ext-Pest does not want to attract the attention of the authorities. But if you go off the grounds, we can't protect you. You had a close call on your way here. Let it humble you, and not embolden you. The EP's are serious and ruthless. And we are all at risk. Not just you. Please remember that." Helen's voice telegraphs through my brain.

I know she's right. But running is all I have. I really need Creature Night and to be training with my team. I need Hasta. The fox runs parallel to me, moving in and out of the shelter of the trees. She risked leaving the safe perimeter to save me. Has she been charged with guarding me? Who told her to watch over me? She put herself in danger for me. I need to be more careful. It's not just my life I'm risking.

I sneak into my room to change out of my wet clothes. I know I'll have to report what happened eventually, but right now I can't bear any more reprimands than those that I am already piling onto myself. I towel-dry my hair and crawl into bed, missing Q, Hasta and, most of all, my mother.

"Helen, I saw something peculiar while you were dancing the other day. I saw . . . light." I'm finishing a third cup of tea in Helen's library. I've been hesitating to mention what I saw, wondering if she is sensitive about it.

"Yes. It's my bioluminescence."

"Like fireflies?"

"Not exactly. It's a metabolic reaction in all humans. When free radicals react with protein and lipids and combine with fluorophores, light is created. I noticed it in my cheeks when I was younger and, at first, thought it was normal blushing. Then I was on a Girl Scout camping trip and we were all around the campfire when my face took on an eerie glow. The scout leader thought I had put on luminescent face paint as a joke. I knew that it was something more, but I played along. Then later, I learned how to generate more and more light and to control it. It's fun and it also keeps the free radicals in my body from causing cell damage and aging."

"So that's your secret."

"Well, health has always been my primary concern, for the planet and for all beings. I'm glad you came today because I have something for you. Your father gave it to me a long time ago and I know he'd want you to have it. I've known it belonged to you ever since you were born, but I couldn't trust the postal service with it. It's too valuable. And besides I think, selfishly, I wanted to give it to you in person."

Helen opens up a rolltop desk and pulls out a small worn paper box that she places in my hand. It carries the same vibration as my father's compass. My antennae have been searching for more of my father's presence in all of the billions of signatures streaming through the Universe. And I send continual signals to him: "I miss you. I want to know you. Where are you now?"

While staring at the box, my scalp tingles and my hair rouses to stand on end. I reach up to try to tame it and Helen puts a strong hand on my shoulder to ground me. As soon as my hair begins to settle down, the box begins shaking in my hand. Is the box moving or is my hand trembling? I set it down on the arm of my chair and while I stare at my steady hand, the box quivers like its cold. I reach over and lift up the lid. Inside is a tin pin, shaped like a bee, inscribed with "Bee Still and Know Thyself." The box stops moving as soon as I lift out the pin.

"He gave this to you?" Tears blur the outline of the bee and I blink hard a few times to clear my vision.

"We each got one at the end of the summer, everyone in camp that year. We didn't know that he had copied the message from the gate leading into the Findhorn garden and then added his own touch to it. He told us that the key to a healthy path through life was to quiet our minds and listen to our inner voices. He was so wise, your father. Like you."

Shaky from adrenaline and emotion, I fumble with the clasp until Helen takes it out of my hands. She pins it on my shirt where I can see it.

"You are your father's and mother's daughter, for sure. Your dedication to Nature and to the bees comes from him and your courage to risk your life to fight for them comes from her."

I touch the pin and my hair rustles and I know that he is here with us. I have a father and he's still working for the Cause and not just through me. The long stream of his being and all that he's done is still in Now. He's an Unseen One. Could he be the Comforter from the Great Hall? Did Abram's music draw him in? Did having his son and daughter together at Findhorn trigger his return? "Helen, do all the Unseen Ones come from another sphere? Could they be loved ones that we lost?"

"I know they come from more boundless realms and territories than we can imagine. I believe your father is still here at the Foundation, guiding us with his knowledge and protecting us with his belief in the restorative capabilities of humans and Nature."

My palm covers the pin and I close my eyes. I hear the door open and close softly. Helen is giving me time with my father. The Comforter reminds me to relax and stay open. My breath stops me from trying too hard and keeps me in Now. "Dad, I'm ready to know you. We need your help."

There she is again, tracking me as I roam further into the heather and rocks north of the settlement. I know foxes from home. And even though we guard the chickens from them, they are not aggressive and usually shy away from humans. This one is different. She's engaging. She's staring at me, pacing back and forth, like she has been waiting for me and I'm late. What is she trying to tell me? I move closer and she watches me, stamping her foot on the ground. Then pacing back and forth, back and forth. I offer her my hand to sniff and she does, inhaling deeply and then, lifting up on her hind legs, she places her front paws on my shoulders. I hold my breath. She smells my neck, jumps down and resumes stamping her foot. I imitate her and stamp my foot. An echo of my stamp resounds beneath us, a hollow sound like a knock on an empty wooden box.

When I kneel down and rap the ground, my knuckles find wooden slats. I wipe away the leaves to uncover a wooden door. The fox nudges me from behind and I turn to look into her eyes. She turns around and shovels leaves and dirt with her hind legs, covering the door once more. It's such a quick turn-around that I'm confused.

What does she want me to do? She wanted me to find the door. She led me to it. She nudges me again, pushing me away from the door. I look at her and try to understand. Where does the door go? If she led me here, why is she sending me away? But she is adamant that I leave. My curiosity is full-blown and I'm caught in my least favorite position of having to wait to know. I want to know about the door. I want to know Now. But Now is leaving the door behind and finishing my run.

During the rest of my run, my thoughts are searching for a handle to lift up the door and discover what's inside. But I keep running, urging my thoughts to merge with Now. Now is the light breeze, the tang of sea air and the rhythm of my shoes on the earth. I know where the door is and I can return there. But I have to wait and trust the fox's timing. Not my own.

"The more sensitive we become . . ."

". . . the more we struggle to keep balanced." Svetlana finishes her sister's sentence and continues. "Now you are teaching us to be even more sensitive. We're afraid of more struggles ahead. How do you do it? How do you keep your center?"

"How do I balance when my world tips and dips under me? If my gift of hypersentience is the problem, then I find a way to use my sensitive nature to solve the problem. The tree pose is one way." Rooting into my standing leg, I lift my other foot to place it against my inner thigh and press my foot and thigh equally to maintain balance. With one outstretched finger, I touch the electrical field around me. Once I anchor my finger into the field, the tree pose stabilizes and I can shut my eyes. As long as I follow my breath, I can hold the pose. If I lose contact with my breath, I wobble and have to open my eyes. Otherwise I am held. Held by the charge around me, held by my focus on Now. After several minutes of balance in stillness, I bring my foot down and face the twins.

Dania has already slipped off her shoes and is shifting her weight onto one foot, raising the other to tuck it inside of her standing leg. She lifts a finger and I watch her plug it into the electrical sheath surrounding her, holding steady as her eyes close. Svetlana hesitantly follows her sister's lead. When her eyes shut, Svetlana loses her balance and quickly opens them again. Even with eyes closed, Dania senses her sister's hesitation and waves her closer, extending the tip of one finger as an anchor. Svetlana regains her pose and, with the touch of her twin's fingertip, finds her balance. They remain, like twin flamingos, breathing in unison. Their calming emanations are contagious and a waft of their contentment washes over me. Thank you, Abram, for bringing me my next mission.

CHAPTER 22

I'M TAKING THE SAME RUN today and will pass by the trapdoor. I've been every day since the fox showed it to me, but something tells me not to venture further unless she appears. She is in charge and I must trust her timing. Waiting is so hard. I hit the trail running hard and my footfall is louder and more weighted than normal. My impatience and irritation are beating the ground beneath me. "I want to know, I want to know," becomes my chant. Not very enlightened or egoless, but at least it's how I honestly feel. Weaving around a few shrubs, I'm within a hundred feet of the door when the fox arrives.

Dropping out of thin air, she suddenly blocks my way and I skid to a stop. I watch her, winded and expectant. She goes to the door and sits beside it. Tentatively, I go to her and kneel down beside her. Ready for anything: exploration or her signal for no entry. She nudges my side and begins to clear the leaves away. I wait to be certain she is ready for me to go forward. She pushes me again, harder this time, and I search around for a handle. I find a groove that fits my hand, lift the door and look down onto a ladder into a small enclosure. The fox urges me again by pressing her nose into my back. I take the ladder slowly, feeling like a trespasser because I am one. Who lives here and why? A troll or goblin? A hermit of the Scottish Highlands? It's a hideaway for someone, someone who befriends foxes.

The ladder takes me to a warren big enough for a very rustic bed but not much else. Wool blankets line the walls and add needed dryness and warmth. At the foot of the bed is a small trunk of necessities including a flashlight, knife, toilet paper, aspirin and a first-aid kit. At the very bottom is a box, taped shut. My hands itch to rip off the tape and learn more. The quarters are lived in and I am an intruder. Somehow a deserted cabin is okay to search, but I'm disturbing a creature's living quarters.

A low growl followed by a whine reaches my ears and I peek above ground at the fox. Anxiously pacing back and forth, she is signaling me to leave. I'm reluctant but quickly recall my directive from my training. The ward is never wrong. And for now, the fox is my ward, or maybe she thinks I'm her ward. Either way, I need to follow her directive. I climb back up the ladder, close the hatch and help her cover the door with leaves. She thanks me with a lick on my cheek. Her first kiss. I scratch behind her ears and watch her saunter off into the brush. I need to know what's in the box. I want to know more about the hermit of the hovel.

I'm glad I agreed to meet the twins at the hives for a lesson. I need the distraction. I want to work with them to practice empathic docking: linking yourself to your empathic mark to learn more about it.

"Last time I explained the long version of Mind Command. Now I'll tell you the shortcut. Find a letter or word that stops you in your tracks. For me, it's just an X. Whatever you choose, that letter or word will be your wake-up call. Make it short and easy to conjure up. When you start down a thought track that is wrong for you and you don't have time to use the tape measure, just use your wake-up signal. Then you're back in Now and can start fresh with a new thought.

"You can't always choose the reality that surrounds you, but you can always choose your thoughts. Watch how changing a thought changes you and your surroundings. You can influence the people around you to help them, and most of all, you stay centered in yourself." A flash of Amey brushing my hair in preparation for my trip reminds me to add, "You can even soothe a crying baby.

"You can also learn to read another being, its moods and intentions, by picking up its unique electrical signature and deciphering it. Every being is constantly sending out signals. For example, I can tell by the electrical charge around a person if they're lying. The constant buzz I normally detect turns into a high-pitched whine. The signals are there if you pay attention to them and use them to help you decide what to do next. Read these signals and you can prevent disasters before they happen. You're equipped already, but not tuned in. Like a radio you've always had in your possession but have never turned on. After you switch it on, listen. The more you listen for the signals, the more signals you receive and can interpret. You can't hear until you listen.

"And if we can pick up signals from people, why not from bees? Bees pick up electrical messages left on flowers by other pollen-gathering bees and can tell the ones that have been recently harvested. They pass those flowers by and find the untouched flowers that are filled with pollen. So why can't I communicate with a pulse that I receive from a bee? How is that so different from the messages from my watch? We know animals exercise this skill constantly without a watch, so why can't we? We are animals, after all."

Dania leans forward and gazes into the hive. "What do the bees want from us?"

"To give them a safe haven and leave them to do the rest. They've lived in trees and hollow logs for millennia. When we listen to them, they'll tell us how to best support them in a changing environment. Clear out mites? They'll tell us how. Regulate the temperature spikes? They'll tell us how. It's a mistake to be fatalistic, with no hope to change the outcome. There's time. Nature is creative and hardy and wants to work with us. She wants to get well. She is wise beyond her years and that's saying a lot since she is very, very old."

As if following a silent command, we all three bow our heads at the same instant, instinctively looking down toward the earth. Our heartbeats join the buzzing of the bees in a synchronized rhythm. Rani alights on my crown. I tell her, "I've missed you,"

Her pacing reminds me of the first day we met. "Shhhhhhhhhh."

It's still early when I leave KP after breakfast prep. My breakfast, an egg sandwich and an apple, is tucked inside a paper bag. My appetite grows the farther I move away from the mess hall and leave the others behind. I want to find a quiet, secluded spot to eat and think. There is a glade of cedars around a small brook that calls to me. I find a warm spot where morning sun offsets the northern wind and I sit in a sunny spot, laying my breakfast beside me. With only birdsong and a murmuring brook as company, I close my eyes and sink into Nature's ambient sound.

I must have nodded off because when I awake the sun has moved, leaving me in the shade. The bag is open and the apple and half of the sandwich are gone. More curious than upset, I look around for a sign of the thief. Suddenly ravenous, I eat the other half of the sandwich. With sustenance, my brain clicks into gear and I know who took the food and where she is.

On the way to the trapdoor, I find her stretched out across the path, licking her chops and waiting for me. I greet her with a ruffling of her fur and a kiss on the top of her head. She gets up lazily, stretches and starts toward the woods, turning back once to see if I'm following her. I am too excited to hope that she is taking me to the lair. I concentrate on using my breath to stay in Now.

When we do arrive, I sit down on the trapdoor to center myself. I so want to rush in and rip open the sealed box but I need to stay in Now. I've been carrying tape with me to reseal the box after I examine it. I reach my hand into my backpack to ensure that the tape is still there. Then I descend the ladder and go straight to the box.

Lifting the tape carefully, I peer into the open box to find a single book: a Gideon Bible that I recognize from our World Religion class. The teacher told us that out in the world they are found in every hotel, restaurant and waiting room. Sometimes it is the only book available to read. Curious, I thumb through it.

The words blur after the first few sentences and I realize I'm crying. But it's not the Bible passages that are making me cry. I remember my mother reading to me from what she called her bible: a book called *Silent Spring*. In beautiful prose Rachel Carson spills out her passion for insect life and her warning and appeal to care for Nature's sensitive balance. I memorized one thought from the Dutch biologist C. J. Briejer quoted in her book and recited it for my mother's birthday when I was eight. She loved it. I remember it still: "The insect world is nature's most astonishing phenomenon. Nothing is impossible to it; the most improbable things commonly occur there. One who penetrates deeply into its mysteries is continually breathless with wonder. She knows that anything can happen, and that the completely impossible often does."

My mother knew that I had replaced 'he' with 'she' and that made her smile. She disappeared only a month after that birthday. My vision is clouded with tears when I turn to put the Bible back into the box, and it drops on the floor. I am cradling it in my hands once again when I spot a tiny yellow paper scroll sticking out from the binding. I coax it out of its hiding place and unroll it. It's a small square, a Post-it, with a child's drawing of a sunflower surrounded by bees. I've seen it before. I recognize it because I drew it.

My heart leaps and I look around with new eyes, trying to find other evidence of my mother. But there's nothing personal here, a lodger that is trying hard to give nothing away. Maybe I've found her. . . or her captor. I push the scroll back inside the bookbinding and quickly retape the box before clamoring up the ladder.

When I come out into the daylight, the fox is waiting, sitting on her haunches and looking pleased with herself as if she'd accomplished a very important task. I am frozen to the spot and giddy, reeling with discovery and brimming with so many questions. Does my mother live here? If not my mother, then who? And why is the fox so keen on my knowing this hideaway? As if knowing I was thinking of her, she turns swiftly and starts kicking leaves and twigs to cover the door. I scoop up more dirt and leaves, and soon the door is gone from sight. My heart flutters with excitement and fear. Should I leave my mother a sign that only she would understand or is it too risky? The fox nudges me away from the door as if to answer my question and I stretch out my palms to thank her. She breathes in my scent through my fingers and I lean down and breathe into her ruff. She smells of parsnip roots and mushroom musk.

She walks beside me until I see the lights of Findhorn and then she's gone as swiftly as she came. I search the landscape, but my eyes cannot follow her retreat. I know that I'll see her again and for now that has to be enough. I don't think I'll sleep tonight.

I do sleep, after all, and I dream about my mother. She's enclosed in a sleeping bag, hanging upside down from the ceiling over my bed. I wake her up by swinging her back and forth gently and calling her name. She gazes at me before turning into a bat and flying past me out of the room. I pull the sleeping bag down and bury myself inside.

When I awaken, my pillow is wet with tears. Rani, sensing my need, has come from her hive and rests on my cheek, crooning to me. I shake off the sadness of my dream. I feel my mother is near, and hope for her return is stronger than I've felt in years. Do I have to hold the discovery of the lair until I know for sure? I want to find my mother more than anything in the world. Is there anyone here that could understand my dream and help me right now? Helen feels too close to confide in and I don't know the twins well enough. Who would understand about both my loss and my secret?

Bertie's kind face suddenly appears in my mind. He knows loss and, as an artist, he is curious and unafraid when it comes to mystery. What if I'm too scared to tell him about my dream and my discovery? I can decide how much to share after I get there. I just know that I don't want to be alone right now. His house is only a few minutes away and when I arrive, I knock tentatively and wait. After several more minutes of knocking and waiting, I press my ear to the thick wooden door and listen for sounds of life. All I can hear is my measured breathing flowing in and out. I knock again, harder this time, and impatient for Bertie to come, I try opening the door. It opens easily and keeping my feet on the outside mat, I call for Bertie. "Bertie? Are you there? Bertie, it's me, Gaia . . . Alexa."

"Bertie! Are you here?" Alarmed by my slip of the tongue, my voice turns shrill and I sound small and desperate. Fragments of my dream replay in my head. I duck inside and follow the hallway to the stairwell and wind my way up to the studio. My art pieces are set neatly in a row and I pick one up. The weight of the baked clay is reassuring, giving me something to hold onto, something solid and reassuring. I set it back in its place and wander around the studio, uncertain of what to do next. I'm searching for something but have no idea what I'm looking for. Even though Bertie isn't here, the room carries his energy and I begin to feel a little better. His space is embracing me as I move among his art.

I stop in front of a bookcase filled with tall sketchbooks, each marked with a date on the spine. I pick out the one dated the year after my mother went missing and I leaf through it. Delicate sketches of flowers and birds in Bertie's fine hand grace each page. Little notes in the margin tell about his discoveries on his nature walks. I return the volume and select one dated last year and turn to the first page, and a portrait of my fox stares back at me. The realization that Bertie has encountered the larger-than-life fox brings the artist's presence fully into the room. Bertie knows my fox. I flip through the rest of the sketches to find her eating an apple right off the tree, chasing a butterfly and even one of her curled up at Bertie's feet by the fire, his familiar slippers warming next to her. Knowing the fox and Bertie are friends softens the edges of my loneliness. I put his sketchbooks away, leaving the studio just as I found it, and slip out the door.

CHAPTER 23

"WHAT DO YOU DO FOR fun around here?"

Dania is restless after several hours of training. Svetlana looks up from her journal writing as if to second her sister's question. I know this is not the fun that they have in mind, but I can't help myself.

"I have an idea. Follow me."

In such a short time I've become so impressed with how hard the twins work and I wish that I had more ways to give them fun. Svetlana is now adept with the bees and is trying out new techniques to help her butterflies. And Dania is focused on the Unseen Ones and spends a lot of her time in the Meditation Hut in the Original Garden. She is calling on them for help with her bees in Vladivostok. I've joined her in her practice several times when the room became so hot with electrical vibration that I had to move into the garden to cool off.

They follow me to the hive and I telepathically reach out to Rani. She comes and nestles in the hollow in my throat. As soon as she settles, the hive is on the move. The swarm is swift and directed and the bees settle on my head, neck and shoulders, crowding together to be near Rani. I remember my mother in her cape of bees. I breathe and find Now. Now is a rhapsody of buzzing and tickling. It's a relief to be out of my small mind and to be in a hive collective. Ensconced in the hive, I relinquish my humanness. I wonder for an instant how my two students are taking this in, and then I forget them and rest in Now.

I'm in the lair and the fox waits for me above. I wasn't expecting to come today. During my run to Cluny Hill, she appeared and stamped her foot and I followed her here. I'm not finding any new clues to the hermit's identity and I can't look at the little bee drawing again without crying. I'm almost ready to climb out when I hear, or rather feel, footsteps overhead. My first thought is that I hope the fox is hidden, and my second is to find a hiding place for myself, which I already know is ridiculous. There's no hiding place in this hiding place. I'm caught, so I stand still and try to look nonthreatening.

The trapdoor lifts up and I hold my breath. I'm more embarrassed than scared, which seems crazy. Feet appear and move down the ladder. Dark boots and long legs. I don't know if I should cough or speak or stay still. I know who I want this to be. I don't wait for a head to appear. "Mother?"

"Gaia!"

The next moments are lost to me in my disbelief, relief, anger, joy and grief. I'm sobbing and laughing at the same time. Each emotion peaks and ebbs rapidly, followed by another just as intense. I'm babbling and moving dizzily through every stage of my childhood that she missed, from petulant nine to arrogant fourteen. "Where have you been? I thought you were dead! I can't believe it's you. How could you? I hate you! I missed you so much. I love you I hate you I love you I love you."

She holds me and gives me time. I cling to her ferociously, as if my life depends on it. I am the baby monkey who grips her mother's fur in flight for fear of falling to the jungle floor below. I'm weak and shaking and I lean into her before realizing that the fox is beside me. I didn't notice her coming down the ladder. Her warm pressure is comforting and I push back, urging her closer. It appears that I have two mothers, one who croons to me and the other who nuzzles me. She presses into me, nestling into my side, while my mother holds me and murmurs in my ear.

"I'm here. I'm here."

I come up for air. Blinking through heavy tears, my mother appears before me in a haze. I've seen her in so many of my dreams in the same mist before she evaporates into thin air. My mother. Can I think that? I hear Quince's voice telling me I have to separate 'my' and 'mother'. My mother hands me a cloth and I wipe my face and scream into the fabric for one last tantrum display. She gently takes it from me and holds me by my shoulders. "I'm so sorry I hurt you."

"I know why you did it. I know you did it to protect me, and all of us. I know that."

"I'm still so sorry. Do you forgive me?"

"Oh, Mother! Don't ask me such a stupid question!" Her serious face gives way and is replaced by the smile I remember and have missed. I suddenly think of the passport with her photo made by someone who knew that she was alive.

"Who knew you were here? Who knew you were still alive?" I am trying to be patient with all of this, but I have no more tolerance left. "Mom? Please! I won't be mad." I say it because I know why she's hesitating, but I don't promise I won't be mad. I am too hurt and confused to promise anything.

"The Commander and Helen knew. I got word to them through the Cause. I told them not to tell anyone, even you, for fear it would put you in danger. Even Hack didn't know. The Commander asked Hack to make up the passport 'just in case' there was a miracle and I turned up."

I thought back to my conversation with the Commander and how she hinted my mother might be near. How could she know and not tell me?

"Don't blame the Commander or Helen. They each said keeping this from you was the hardest thing they ever had to do. I made them promise and told them both I would break off all contact if they told you. I gave them no choice."

My mother had to separate from me to do what was best for everyone. I know her and it was probably the hardest thing she ever did. I sink back into her arms, pressing my cheek against her breast.

"Gaia, what can I do to help you?"

"Just hold me and tell me about the fox."

Her voice goes soft with sentiment. It's the same voice she used when she told me stories about the Cause. The comforting thrum of her voice resonates through her chest into my head.

"After I went underground, I was heartsick missing everyone, and most especially you. The first week, I cried myself to sleep every night. On the eighth night, a strange cry in the woods woke me from a fitful sleep. It sounded like a newborn baby. I followed the mewing and there she was, a little rag of fur. She was no more than a few days old, eyes closed and with barely the strength to cry out. Wet, cold and hungry. Before I put her inside my coat to warm her, I looked all around for her mother but couldn't find her. I carried her to my room and fed her with a milk-soaked washcloth. She suckled wildly and purred herself to sleep.

I went out for ten days after that and searched again for the mother. But I never found any sign of her, alive or dead. Vixen has been with me ever since."

"Ohhh, Vixen is her name. Did you know she's been following me? And I think she saved my life."

"No, I knew she was busy doing something, but I had no idea she was tracking you. Thank goodness she did!"

I lift up my head and turn toward Vixen who is now curled up between us. "She led me here, to you. She must have sensed you knew me."

"I talked about you enough! Vixen has heard a lot of stories about the Compound. No one knew where I was staying, except her. Well, no one did until now."

She smiles at me and pulls my head back onto her chest. I rest there and breathe her in. We need to figure out what to do next. It's not safe for either of us to return to the Compound. "Mom, we can't go back to the Compound. Not now. They're looking for me."

"I know." The look my mother turns on me is full of longing. Unconsciously, she reaches out a hand to caress Vixen, who starts to purr.

"Mom, Bertie, the potter, knows Vixen. He makes sketches of her and she visits him in his house. I think they are very good friends."

"Why are you telling me this, Gaia?"

"Because we can leave here and go somewhere. I have a passport for you. But I don't want you to worry about Vixen being alone. She'll have Bertie. Mom, what do you want to do?"

"I want time with my daughter and I want to help. I'm tired of hiding and living underground. I want to work for the Cause again. I want to start another sanctuary somewhere where I'm needed, like before."

Bright flashes of Dania and Svetlana busily working at the hives blind me for an instant.

"Mom?"

"Yes, Gaia."

"Do you know any Russian?"

POSTSCRIPT

Hack, Mom and I leave today, thanks to your packet of goodies. Please get this to Abram. We'll be in touch. Love, G.

Abram, this is your little sis. I'm back with my mom. We're going away together and I don't want you to worry about me. And I'm going to tell you a secret. My name isn't really Alexa, it's Gaia. Like the Earth goddess. You knew that somehow. I don't know how we know these things, but we do. And I'm glad you sensed my real name, because now I know you'll be able to hear me, no matter where you are. And I will always be listening for "Gaia's Song."

I do all of this for Her. For our Mother, the Earth.

I love you, Gaia

THE END

WHAT CAN YOU DO TO HELP?

The environmental crisis is forever on my mind, tugging at me to figure out a way to help as one small being on the planet. "What can I do to help?" spurred me on to meet Gaia and write her story. I want to encourage all of you to find a way to write, draw, paint, build, sculpt, dance, speak or sing your answer to the question. Creativity and Art are healing modalities that penetrate even the most stuck mind or situation.

WHAT ELSE CAN YOU DO?

- Play in the dirt. Dig and plant seeds.
- Plant butterfly weed and other plants that bees and butterflies and other insects need for food or nesting.
- Feed the birds.
- Get a rain barrel and use it for watering.
- Get binoculars to see up close the amazing creatures in your garden.
- Spend 20 minutes gazing at a small patch of earth and discover Nature's treasures.
- Get to know a tree. Spend time with it, hug it and talk to it. Trees love to share their rootedness and bring grounding and security to a rocking and rolling world. You are visiting your original deeper roots, for we come from the soil and return to it.

TOOLS FOR MANAGING FEAR, ANXIETY and DEPRESSION ABOUT OUR WORLD

Sometimes it's very hard to be an Earthling, especially if you are sensitive and aware. Here's a list of my favorite remedies for sanity. Try one out, and if it doesn't suit you, throw it out and try another one. Invent your own and share them with others.

- Check out somatic work and polyvagal therapy. Make a polyvagal map and study your nervous system and its unique functions.
- List your fears, dreams, wishes, desires. Whatever you feel or think is always worthy of noting. And it helps to write them down

and study them. Fears can be processed and released and dreams and wishes can be realized with first steps.

- Watch and record your night dreams. You are having precognitive dreams and message dreams that can help you heal yourself and the planet. By paying attention to them you can learn more about yourself. Find a dream group or therapist to help.
* We all have a part in healing the world. We can't do it all, just our piece. Find out what your piece is and start moving toward it. It could be making an art project, joining an environmental group, starting a book club about climate change, giving five dollars to help the Monarch butterfly or the bees, taking a walk or visiting with Unseen Ones. You are the only one with that particular purpose. It is yours and yours alone. When each one of us does our little piece, we make a great team.
- And listen to Now and know your breath is your most valuable ally. Befriend it and you can find your center even in the toughest of times.

Remember that every emotion boils down to either Love or Fear. And the ultimate antidote to Fear is to turn toward Love.

It's important to first acknowledge, feel and release any anger and frustration. All feelings have equal rights! I like to write it out, rip magazines, draw an angry picture or pound a pillow. After honoring and releasing the anger, it's easier to get to the love.

Send love to the people who are damaging the
Earth, to the Ext-Pests of our world.
They need our love to conquer their fear.
Use Love in Action to fight for the world you want.